MW00941328

So

Happy

Together

By:

Brooke St. James

No part of this book may be used or reproduced in any form or by any means without prior written permission of the author.

Copyright © 2017

Brooke St. James

All rights reserved.

Other titles available from Brooke St. James:

Another Shot:
A Modern-Day Ruth and Boaz Story

When Lightning Strikes

Something of a Storm (All in Good Time #1)
Someone Someday (All in Good Time #2)

Finally My Forever (Meant for Me #1)
Finally My Heart's Desire (Meant for Me #2)
Finally My Happy Ending (Meant for Me #3)

Shot by Cupid's Arrow

Dreams of Us

Meet Me in Myrtle Beach (Hunt Family #1)
Kiss Me in Carolina (Hunt Family #2)
California's Calling (Hunt Family #3)
Back to the Beach (Hunt Family #4)
It's About Time (Hunt Family #5)

Loved Bayou (Martin Family #1)
Dear California (Martin Family #2)
My One Regret (Martin Family #3)
Broken and Beautiful (Martin Family #4)
Back to the Bayou (Martin Family #5)

Almost Christmas

JFK to Dublin (Shower & Shelter Artist Collective #1)
Not Your Average Joe (Shower & Shelter Artist Collective #2)
So Much for Boundaries (Shower & Shelter Artist Collective #3)
Suddenly Starstruck (Shower & Shelter Artist Collective #4)
Love Stung (Shower & Shelter Artist Collective #5)
My American Angel (Shower & Shelter Artist Collective #6)

Summer of '65 (Bishop Family #1)
Jesse's Girl (Bishop Family #2)
Maybe Memphis (Bishop Family #3)

Chapter 1

Daniel Bishop
Orlando, Florida

Daniel Bishop was only fifteen years old when he started training with his Uncle Gray at Alpha Security. That was nearly a decade ago, and now Daniel was an integral part of the business and had plans to eventually become a partner.

Daniel's grandfather, Michael Bishop, was the founder and CEO of Bishop Motorcycles, which meant that Daniel was born into a life of freedom and luxury. He had shares in the company and could have easily settled into being a silent partner in the family motorcycle business, but instead, he joined his uncle at Alpha Security.

Alpha was based in Memphis, Tennessee, but Gray Kennedy provided training and placement for elite-level personal security all over the world. He was ex-military and had just the right kind of specialized training to equip the best bodyguards in the business.

He started by training bodyguards for famous actors and musicians, but over the years, his reputation had opened doors with the Secret Service and other, more official types of security. He now had men in important positions all over the world.

Alpha Security took pride in training the best of the best.

The initial training camp lasted roughly two years and was highly intensive. The trainees lived onsite, and by the time they had completed the process, they were legitimately lethal weapons. They were capable of handling crisis situations and protecting their clients, but they also had integrity and impeccable manners, which was what set Gray's program apart from others of its kind. Gray knew his men would be a major part of their clients' lives, so they were trained to not only be protectors but also companions.

Daniel was only a teenager when he began training at Alpha, so he had gone through the program a few times over and was now an instructor. He didn't begin his journey at Alpha with the intention of working as a bodyguard, however—the whole thing was more of a family intervention.

Gray had told Daniel that he was "big for his age" and would be "the ideal bodyguard when he got old enough", but all that was just a way to convince him to begin the program. As a teenager, Daniel had shown signs of self-destructive behavior; so basically, his Uncle Gray was just giving him the opportunity to get involved with the intention of trying to keep him out of trouble.

Gray's plan was a complete success.

In the years since Daniel had begun the program, he had not only managed to stay out of trouble, but had also been molded into an intelligent warrior and leader who was capable of training and inspiring other men. Daniel was an important part of Gray's team, and both of them were grateful for the way things had played out.

This weekend, however, Daniel was not in Memphis training and inspiring at Alpha Security. In fact, he didn't feel much like a warrior at all as he stood on the sidelines of his sister's gymnastics tournament, holding a bag that reeked of perfume and was full of sparkly things and hair products.

Orlando, Florida (and Disney specifically) was a vacation destination for most people, but Gray was there for only one reason, and that was to support his 17-year-old sister, Ivy, as she competed with her gymnastics team.

Their mother, Rose, had come on the trip as well. The two women could have, no doubt, made the trip on their own, but Ivy begged Daniel to come, saying that she didn't have plans to continue with the sport after high school and this would be one of her very last meets. She also mentioned that she and the other girls on the team needed protection since they were in a tourist town and there were probably villains waiting around every corner to take advantage of young, unsuspecting women.

Needless to say, Ivy knew how to push Daniel's buttons, and now he found himself playing the role of 'team brother' while they competed in the meet. Ivy's coach was a family friend of theirs, so at Ivy's request, Daniel had been given an all-access pass to go down on the floor with the girls during the competition.

He had been to a couple of these tournaments when Ivy was younger, but never one of this magnitude. From a security standpoint, he was actually glad he had decided to come with them. He found himself on the sidelines, scanning the audience and making sure everyone was safe.

Ivy's team was doing their vault routines when Daniel's phone vibrated in his pocket. He took it out and looked at it, noticing that there was a missed call from his uncle. He was still looking at the screen when a text came in.

Gray: "Call me ASAP!"

Gray was not one to overreact or be dramatic, so Daniel knew it must be serious. His sister was sitting a few feet away with the other girls on her team, and he crossed over to her, handing her the duffle bag.

"Where are you going?" she asked with a curious expression.

"I have to call Uncle Gray," he said.

He was somewhat aware of the fact that several of the girls on the team had crushes on him—most of Ivy's friends did—it just worked out that way with their age difference and the fact that Daniel was a big, tough guy. They all tried their best to get his attention, and usually Daniel would smile or be polite to them, but this time, he stayed focused on his sister.

"Did you see my vault?" she asked.

He smiled and nodded. "Good job," he said. "Proud of you."

"Are you coming right back?" she asked.

He nodded again as he walked away.

Daniel made his way off of the mats, heading toward the concession area. He glanced at his mom on his way out and noticed that she was preoccupied talking to some of the other parents in the stands. He dialed the number and put the phone to his ear as soon as he was able to hear his call.

"Daniel?" Gray said, picking up on the first ring.

"Yeah, what's up? Is everything okay?"

"I'm glad you called me back. We've got a problem down in Miami. Trevor Bailey's sick. He's in the hospital with a high fever. They're running tests on him."

"I'm sorry," Daniel said. "What can I do to help?"

"You can fill in for him tomorrow. His client has some press engagements followed by a concert."

Daniel was perfectly capable of doing the job, but he cringed at the thought of it. There was a reason he was an instructor rather than a bodyguard—he would much rather work with the staff of Alpha Security than with the stars they protected. He knew he had the skillset to fill in for Trevor, but he really wasn't looking forward to it.

"What about Nick?" he asked after a few seconds of contemplation.

"Nick's not ready for a job like this," Gray said.

Daniel knew Gray was right. For the past few years, Trevor Bailey had been providing personal security to the ultra-famous, blonde bombshell Courtney Cole. She was the definition of a pop princess. Trevor was amazing at his job—a solid-rock of a man—smart, quick, and extremely dangerous in a confrontation, which was exactly what was needed for a job of this caliber.

"What about James?" Daniel asked.

"James would do it, but he just left for Japan with John Mayer."

Daniel thought of asking about Hank, Charles, or Michael, but he could tell his uncle wanted him to do the job. He took a deep breath. "Miami?" he asked.

"Yes," Gray said. "That's why I called you. I knew you were already down there in Florida. It's only about a four-hour drive from Orlando, and we don't need you there till first thing in the morning. I figured that gave you plenty of time to finish what you're doing with Ivy."

Daniel was quiet for so long that Gray added, "She's only got two more dates on this tour—New Orleans and Dallas. If Trevor's still sick, we can get someone else to fill in for the other two. It'll just really help us out if you can cover Miami."

"Sure," Daniel said even though it was the last thing he wanted to do.

"Great. Thank you. I wouldn't ask if we weren't in a bind."

"I know," Daniel said.

"You need to be at her hotel by eight tomorrow morning. She's got to be somewhere before noon, and it's gonna be a little bit of a hassle getting her over there. I'll email you with the details."

"Okay."

"Thank you," Gray said.

"No problem."

"Seriously, I know you don't want to do it. I really appreciate it."

"It's fine," Daniel said. "It'll be good."

The gentlemen hung up, and Daniel put his phone in his pocket. As he headed back towards the main auditorium, he felt a pang of dread begin to build in his gut. He loved working with the guys and training them, but honestly, he didn't care for working one-on-one with clients—especially one as high profile as Courtney Cole. It was fine, though, it was just one day of his life, and sometimes you just have to take one for the team.

"What did Uncle Gray need?" Ivy asked as Daniel approached.

Their team was now finished with the vault and everyone was just sitting around, waiting to be called to the next event.

"He asked me to do some work," Daniel said.

Ivy gave him a curious expression. She knew her brother was reluctant to give details, so it was an expression she wore all the time when she was around him.

"He needs me to do a job—to fill in for a guy who got sick."

"You mean as a bodyguard?" she asked.

He nodded.

"I thought you didn't do that."

"I don't, normally."

"So, why are you this time?"

"Because it's a big job, and the guy got sick," Daniel said.

"When is it?"

"Tomorrow, but I'll leave tonight."

"Where do you have to go?"

"Why so many questions?"

"Because I want you to stay for the awards ceremony. I might place on floor."

"I'll stay to see you get your ribbon," he said. "I don't have to leave till later tonight. Uncle Gray said it's only a four-hour drive."

"Where is it?"

"Miami."

"Who are you working for?"

"Some singer."

"Is he famous?"

"She, and yes."

"How famous?" Ivy asked.

"Very."

"Who is it, Daniel?"

"That Cole girl."

"Courtney?" Ivy asked, looking utterly stupefied. "Courtney Cole?"

Daniel looked around with an expression that hinted to Ivy to keep her voice down.

"Courtney Cole?" she whispered in an urgent tone.

He gave her a nod.

"You're doing security for *Courtney Cole*? Are you kidding me right now?"

He shook his head.

"You're lying," she said, pushing at his shoulder.

"I wish I was," he said seriously.

Ivy took a hold of her brother's arm, squeezing it so hard that he looked at her with a disapproving expression.

"You *have* to take me with you!" she whispered. She looked over her shoulder at the other girls before focusing on Daniel again. "Britney, too," she said. "Britney would flip if she knew I got to meet Courtney Cole and didn't take her."

Daniel let out a humorless laugh. "You're not coming with me, and your friend's surely not. *I* don't even want to go on this job. Her normal guy got sick, and I'm filling in for one day."

"Do you get to go backstage?" she asked.

Daniel looked at her as if she should know better than to ask such a question.

"You *have* to take me," she said. "I'll never ask you for anything again in my whole life, but Daniel, you have to do it. You've been working with Uncle

Gray forever, and you *never* go on jobs. All of your guys work with these awesome people, and I *never* get to meet any of them. Courtney Cole is my very favorite singer, Daniel, and you know it. She's the one I went to see in Nashville a few years ago with Britney. We had to sit in the nosebleed section. Please, Daniel, I promise I'll stay out of your way. I'll sit in the corner and let you do your job. You won't even know I'm there. I'll just sit over by the wardrobe person. I'll help. I'll do grunt work. People always need help with grunt work."

Ivy's expression was so genuinely heartbroken at the thought of being left out that Daniel found himself actually thinking about it. He knew it was completely unprofessional and would never have thought about it under normal circumstances, but the circumstances weren't really normal with Trevor's unexpected absence and everything. Plus, Daniel had a guilt-driven soft spot for his siblings that made it almost impossible for him to say 'no' to any of them. He did not want to do the job in the first place, much less take on the added pressure of babysitting his little sister. But he looked at her pleading expression and remembered how short life was and how bad he would feel if he let her down and then never had the chance to make it up to her.

Daniel felt the dread that had been building inside of him begin to grow as he contemplated taking Ivy along.

She could see his expression change as he began to consider it, and she reached out and squeezed him tightly.

"I didn't agree to it," he said.

"I know, but you're thinking about it."

Chapter 2
Courtney

"How's Trevor doing?"

It was the first question I asked when I opened my eyes that morning. No one answered because my words came out sleepily and way too quiet for anyone to hear from the other room. My assistant, Denise, was in the living room of my suite along with my stage manager, Vick.

I hated to be alone, so I always had someone in my room, even if it wasn't right there in the bedroom with me. My mom toured with me for the first few years, but it stressed her out to see me stressed out all of the time, so she had long since been staying home with my step-dad while I went on the road.

Usually, I could count on Denise and Trevor being close by, but this morning, there would be no Trevor. I could see Denise and Vick from my spot on the bed, but my bedroom door was mostly closed, and neither of them knew I was awake. I rolled over, taking my phone off of my nightstand so that I could text her rather than yelling out.

Me: "How's Trevor?"

There was more light in the living room than there was in my room, so I could clearly see Denise as she looked at her phone and then directly toward me. She stood up, smiling as she walked my way.

"Are you really texting me from in here?" she asked with a smile as she came into my room. She stood near the doorway, trying to focus on me even though it was still dark in my room.

"I tried to holler at you, and you didn't hear me," I said sleepily.

"I'm in here talking to Vick. He's about to head downstairs to get some coffee."

"How's Trevor?" I asked.

I was worried about him. He was not only my personal security, but in the years since he had been with me, he had become one of my dearest friends. He had literally never missed a show, and I knew if he went to the hospital it was bad.

"He's fine," she said.

"Fine like he'll be at the show tonight?" I asked.

She smiled. "No, but fine like they're gonna figure it out. Fine like you shouldn't be worrying about it. You've got three shows to go. Let's just chill and focus on finishing them up."

"Who's gonna work security?" I asked.

"She's up if you wanna head down there and get coffee. A grande latte with one pump of simple syrup." Denise had turned to talk to Vick for a second before looking at me again. She sighed. "We contacted Trevor's firm and asked for a sub. They sent a guy named Daniel. He's here. I met him a few minutes ago. He seems like he knows what he's doing. He's a lot like Trevor except quieter."

16

Denise began to open the curtains in my room, and when she did, light spilled in and caused me to squint.

"How'd you sleep?" she asked.

"Okay," I said. "I'm nauseated."

"You're nauseated everyday," she returned, meaning it as an encouragement.

"I know, but I'm extra nauseated today. I was up last night worrying about Trevor. I wonder what's wrong with him."

"You can't worry about that. He's going to be fine. You just have to try to forget about it and get through these last three shows."

I glanced at the clock by my bedside. I had already looked at it, but for some reason the time hadn't registered. I sat up, stretching and yawning when I realized it was almost 8:30. Denise walked around my room, absentmindedly straightening things up.

"You need to hop up. Nina and Jake are here to get you dressed and do your hair and makeup. We have to leave in about an hour."

I groaned as I stood up, feeling like I wanted nothing more than to lay in bed for the next month.

"Come on," she said. "Vick will be back in a minute with coffee."

"I need a shower," I said. I lifted my arm and gave my armpit a sniff, trying to decipher whether or not I could get by without taking one. "I woke up sweating a bunch last night, "I said.

Denise patted me on the back. "You're just worried about Trevor, but he'll be fine, I promise. I'm sure it's just the flu. We were all exhausted after the East Coast. We just have to push through these last few dates."

This type of encouragement was commonplace in my hotel rooms. I was great once we got to the venue, but my nights were predictably rough, and I often needed encouragement to get out of bed. Truth be told, I was not built for life on the road. I loved making music in the studio, but I honestly didn't love the pressures of touring—at least not at the sold-out arena level.

At first, it was a rush to hear people in the audience screaming for me, but the physical symptoms I experienced as a result of the pressure outweighed that rush a long time ago. I suffered from stomach issues that never seemed to resolve in spite of the fact that I had been performing at this level for the last seven years of my life. Touring made me physically ill, but I pushed through it because going on the road was the primary way musicians made a living.

It wasn't only my living at stake either, but literally hundreds of people (including Denise, Vick, Trevor, Nina, Jake, and all of my dancers, band, and stage crew). They were all counting on me to earn an income. If it were just about me, I would have most assuredly quit touring years ago. I was good at saving money, and I had earned enough of it in my career to retire.

Vick was already there with my coffee by the time I got out of the shower and joined Denise and the others in the living room. She thrust the paper cup into my hand as soon as I entered the room. She did it in a rushed way that let me know they had been waiting on me and I should go ahead and sit down in the stylist's chair.

Nina was busy fiddling with setting up her make up station, and Jake was straightening the clothing selections that were hanging on the rack near the chair. Everything seemed to be in order except for the two new faces in the room—one of which I assumed was Trevor's replacement.

"Court, this is Daniel from Alpha Security and his little sister, Ivy." Denise said.

Daniel smiled and gave me a little wave. He was a strikingly handsome man whose presence made me sit up a little straighter. He was thick, but not in a beefy, bodyguard way. He had dark features, was tall with broad shoulders, and had a relaxed, easy manner. He wore casual smile, but the girl she described as his little sister would barely look at me. She seemed shy and nervous, but she managed to give me a slight smile when she saw that I was looking at her.

"Daniel and Ivy were on vacation at Disney when he got the call to come sub for Trevor," Jake explained. He walked over to the girl and patted her on the back as I got settled in my chair and took a sip of my coffee. "We ran into them downstairs, and she's just the sweetest little thing," Jake continued as if taking up for the girl. "She was planning on staying in her hotel room all day today while her brother was busy with you, but I told her she could hang out with me and Nina—be our little apprentice."

I glanced at the girl again, and she smiled shyly like she was trying not to inconvenience me.

"Aren't you a little old for Disney?" I asked, teasing her.

"She had a gymnastics tournament at their sports complex," Daniel said, taking up for his little sister.

His comment made me glance at him.

"I was just messing with her anyway," I said. "You're never too old for Disney."

Nina draped a cape around my neck and instantly went to work on my hair.

"We didn't go to the theme park," Ivy said. "We just went to the competition and then came straight here." Ivy glanced at her brother before lowering her gaze as if assuming that she should remain quiet.

"How did you do at the competition?" I asked.

"I got third place with my floor routine," she said.

"That must have been pretty exciting," I said.

She nodded. "It was for me," she said. "A couple of the other girls on my team placed higher in different events, but I was happy to get a medal at all—especially at such a big meet."

"I love watching gymnastics," I said as Nina continued fussing over my hair. "But the only time I ever get to watch it is when the Olympics are on."

Jake and Nina both agreed that they also enjoyed it and only ever watched it during the Olympics.

"I'm not going to do it in college or anything," Ivy said.

"What are you going to do?" I asked.

"I haven't really figured it out. My family owns a motorcycle shop, so I'll probably just work for them until I decide."

"Motorcycles, huh?" I asked, raising my eyebrows with an impressed smile. I glanced at her brother who wore a serious expression like he wasn't quite sure what to think about his little sister chatting it up with me. "Do you ride a motorcycle?" I asked, looking directly at him.

"No," he said seriously.

"Their last name is Bishop," Jake said. "Daniel and Ivy Bishop. Their grandfather is the guy who started the *Bishop Motorcycle Company*."

"Are you serious?" I asked.

The girl smiled and nodded, but I focused on her brother who was just sitting there taking everything in. "And you don't ride?" I asked him.

"No ma'am, I don't." he said in a matter-of-fact tone.

"Why not?" I asked.

He gave me a little shrug while maintaining a serious demeanor. "I just don't want to," he said.

"Did you ever hear of a blues singer named Ivy Bishop?" Jake asked.

"Yes," I said. I glanced at the girl who had already been introduced as Ivy. I felt somewhat confused since I thought the blues singer in question was popular in the sixties. "Were you named after her or something?"

She nodded. "She's my grandma," Ivy said.

"So, the singer is the same Bishop as the motorcycles?" I asked, feeling a little perplexed.

Jake let out a laugh. "That's the same thing I asked when she told me," he said. "Can you believe it? Same people."

I looked at Daniel, wishing he would add something to the conversation, but he just sat there, surveying the scene.

"Are you telling me that the blues singer, Ivy Bishop, also started a motorcycle company?" I asked.

"It was my grandpa, Michael, who started the motorcycle business." Ivy said.

"And you don't ride one?" I asked, looking at them with a doubtful expression.

"I do," Ivy said. "It's just Daniel who doesn't. I got my first motorcycle before I even got a car."

I glanced at Daniel who seemed content to sit there and not say a word. He certainly was quiet. He was being too professional if you asked me. I wanted him to talk to me the way his sister was doing.

"And what do you do?" I asked him.

"I work at Alpha Security," he answered simply. He wasn't trying to be rude, but his direct answer made me feel like I had asked an obvious question.

I squinted at him. "What do you do *for fun*?" I asked.

"I'm not much on fun," he said. He offered me the slightest hint of a smile, but I could tell there was an underlying seriousness to his answer.

I glanced at his sister who nodded at me. "He's being serious," she said. "But he's sweet. He'd give you the shirt off his back."

"I guess the world needs more people who would do that," I said, "Even if they don't like having fun."

Denise had been engaged in a conversation with Jake during this part of the exchange, but they must have tuned in because Jake said, "I don't know *anyone* who doesn't like to have fun!"

"Me neither," I said, teasing Daniel.

"Who in the world doesn't like to have fun?" Denise asked, obviously missing what we had just said.

I glanced at Ivy, expecting her to chime in, but she just glanced at her brother with a sweet half smile.

I barely knew them and I liked them already. I could tell they cared about each other, and I could see simply by the expression on their faces that they had one another's backs. It was moments like these when I wished I wasn't an only child.

Chapter 3

I had an absolutely crazy day in Miami.

I had two television interviews followed by a radio interview and a photo shoot. Normally, I was able to squeeze in an hour or two of down time before I had to make my way to the arena for sound check, but that wasn't the case in Miami. My whole afternoon was go, go, go, and the next thing I knew, I was getting hair and makeup done for the show.

I missed having my right-hand man, Trevor, by my side, but Daniel Bishop had done an excellent job filling in for him. He was courteous, protective, and all the things that Trevor was. The only difference was that Daniel was extremely quiet and didn't seem impressed by me at all.

He wasn't impolite, but he certainly didn't go out of his way to make me feel like I had hung the moon (which was somehow simultaneously refreshing and heartbreaking). He was so stoic that multiple times throughout the day I had caught myself being goofy and trying to make him smile just because I wanted to see him do it like one of those British soldiers. He would offer me a courtesy grin, but it was obvious that he was there to do the job of protecting me rather than being distracted with becoming my friend.

We were at the arena for about seven hours. The actual show didn't last that long, of course, but a lot went into it, and I was always really exhausted by the time we left. My set list for this tour had twenty-two songs with four wardrobe changes, and I poured every last ounce of energy I had into it. The show had been over for an hour by the time we left the arena, and fans were still standing by the loading dock, waiting to catch a glimpse of me getting into the limo. I could tell Daniel and Trevor had been trained by the same people because Daniel handled the situation just like Trevor would have done, ushering me into the back of the car with quick precision.

He and I were the only two in the back seat on the trip from the arena to the hotel, and I stared straight ahead replaying moments of the concert and thinking about things I should have done differently.

Daniel's hand was resting on his thigh, and I glanced down at it, feeling an odd sense of longing and maybe a little attraction toward him. In my tired haze, I began to compare him to Trevor, and I wondered why I was attracted to him when I had never felt that way toward Trevor.

I stared at his hand. If he were Trevor, he would've put his arm around me instead of keeping it to himself. Longing for the touch and reassurance that Trevor normally provided after a show, I leaned over and rested my head on Daniel's shoulder.

"The show went well," he said.

He smelled different than Trevor. Trevor always smelled like cologne, whereas Daniel smelled

masculine and woodsy, but in a more natural way—
it was almost like I had to get right next to him to
even tell that he smelled at all. Once I did, I found
out that it was really worth it.

"Thank you," I said. "Where's your sister?"

"With Nina," he said.

"Did they go back to the hotel?"

"Yes."

"I think she had fun backstage," I said, hoping I
could make him say more than two words to me if I
continued talking about his sister.

"She did."

He sat up and shifted, glancing out of the back
window, checking our surroundings and making sure
we weren't being followed.

"Did you like the show?" I asked.

"Yes ma'am."

A few seconds of silence passed.

"Why didn't you tell me that?"

"I did," he said.

"No, you didn't."

"I'm sorry. I don't think I understand what you're
saying."

"You said the show went well, but you didn't say
that you liked it."

"I thought that was the same thing."

"No, it's not."

"Well, I liked it," he said.

"Why do you seem so unimpressed?"

"I'm not unimpressed, I'm just trying to do my job—keep you safe. I didn't think you were interested in my opinion. I did like it. You did a good job. I liked how you got everybody pumped up backstage before the show. I've never seen anybody do that."

"Did you like the gold outfit?" I asked.

I regretted it the instant came out of my mouth. I knew it made me sound desperate. The gold outfit I was referring to was a barely-there sequin number, which all the guys seemed to love on account of how little of my skin it covered. I only brought it up because I was desperate to get a rise out of him and I didn't know how else to do it. I had been trying in different, more subtle ways all day with no success, so the comment about the gold outfit was sort of a last-ditch effort.

"That was my least favorite outfit, if you want to know the truth."

His words caused a stabbing sensation in my chest, and I cringed inwardly at the feeling of rejection.

"Thanks a lot," I said sarcastically.

"I'm not trying to be mean, it's just that outfits like that cause men feel a certain way, and from a security standpoint, those are the types of feelings I like to avoid."

He used the opportunity to glance out the window again as if to prove his point. "Men already feel that way about you, even when you're all covered up with clothes."

"So, you're saying they don't need the encouragement of the gold outfit?" I asked.

"No, they don't."

"What about you?"

"What about me?"

"How do you feel about me?"

"You're a beautiful woman."

"Are you married?" I asked.

"No."

"I didn't see a ring, but I thought you must be married because of what a gentleman you are."

He didn't say anything after that. I didn't ask him any more questions, but I thought he would make small talk like Trevor, and he didn't. I laid my head on his shoulder and we rode in silence for a few minutes until we finally pulled up at the hotel.

Daniel put his arm around me and walked me inside in the practiced way of a true professional. We were the only two in the elevator as we rode upstairs.

"I've got a room right next to yours," he said. "Denise said I could stay in your suite since Trevor had a bedroom in there, but I've got Ivy with me, and we're already settled in our room. Denise wrote my number down so you would have it. I have a key to your suite. Just give me a call if you need anything tonight."

"Nina and them are coming up to my room to hang out for a little while before we go to bed," I said. "I told your sister she could come by."

"That was nice of you, but she's too young for that."

"What do you mean, she's too young?"

"She's not of age. She can't be partying."

I felt offended by his words, like he thought I was some drug addict and he didn't want his little sister hanging around me.

"We're not partying," I said. "We're just hanging out and talking and decompressing for a little while because otherwise it's hard for me to go to sleep."

He glanced at me, and his expression softened when he saw that I was a little offended. "I'm sure she would really love to hang out," he said. "Thank you for including her."

Daniel came into my room before he went to his own. He swept the place more thoroughly than Trevor ever did, looking under beds, in closets, on the patio, and even on the rooftop access by the pool. It took him ten minutes. "I'll be right next door," he said when he was satisfied that the place was safe.

I smiled. "Thank you," I said. "You did a good job even though you're not quite Trevor."

He smiled at that. "Thank you."

***

It was customary after every show for a few people to come to my room to hang out and talk or watch TV. We never talked about the performance—

30

we just hung out and pretended like we were normal people who weren't in a different city every night.

I was happy that Ivy had come that evening, and not just because she was a nice girl. It was also because I was intrigued by Daniel and secretly wanted to get more information about him.

Miami was a beautiful city, and the panoramic view of the Atlantic Ocean from my penthouse suite was breathtaking, even at night. It was hot out, so everyone was hanging out in the living room, but Ivy went onto the patio, and after a minute, I followed her. She was looking down at her phone when I came outside, and she quickly put it in her pocket before turning to smile at me.

"I didn't mean to interrupt you," I said.

"You didn't," she said. "I just came out here to text my brother. He was checking on me."

"That's sweet of him," I said. I came to stand next to her at the edge of the balcony. It was warm out, but the wind was blowing, and I took a long slow breath in through my nose, taking in the salty ocean air. "The ocean is good for you," I said.

"I'm gonna try to go for a swim tomorrow before we leave," Ivy said. "Daniel said he doesn't think we'll have time, but I'll end up talking him into it if we get up early enough."

"We'll definitely have time for a swim," I said. "We have the day off tomorrow. We're not leaving for New Orleans until after dinner, I think."

"Yeah, but we're going back to Memphis—me and Daniel. I think our flight's at noon or one. Daniel said something about his replacement being here in the morning."

I literally felt sick at the mention of Daniel leaving. I already lived my life on the verge of being nauseous, anyway, and the news of him leaving after only one day made me feel rejected and heartbroken.

"Does your brother not like me or something?" I asked.

Ivy glanced at me with a concerned expression. "Who, Daniel?"

"Yes."

"No, no, no, he likes you. I think he knew he was only filling in for one day while they found a more permanent solution. Daniel doesn't usually work with clients. He normally stays home in Memphis and trains the guys at Alpha rather than going on the road. He just did this because we were right there in Orlando."

"What if I want him to stay with me until Trevor gets back?" I asked. "I'm the one paying for it. What if I don't want another substitute?"

Ivy shrugged innocently and made a face like she didn't really want to get involved. "I know Daniel doesn't normally work with clients," she repeated.

"Does he not like me?" I repeated, feeling hurt.

"No, he likes you a lot," she said.

"Why doesn't he act like it? He barely says more than two words to me."

"That's just Daniel. He's quiet. He's always like that. He carries a lot of stuff around with him."

"Like what?"

Ivy paused for a second and then looked over her shoulder, hesitating as if she thought her brother might hear her.

"Don't tell anybody I told you this," she whispered.

I nodded.

"He and my brother, Owen, had an accident when we were younger. I was just a little kid. Daniel and Owen were in middle school."

"What happened?"

"They took one of my dad's motorcycles without permission. Daniel was twelve. He was driving, and they had a really bad accident. Nobody died or anything, but Owen got hurt really bad. He's got a pretty noticeable scar all down the side of his face, and he has a fake leg."

"A fake leg?" I asked, thinking I hadn't heard her correctly. I glanced at her and she nodded, looking over her shoulder again.

"His right leg," she whispered. "He doesn't have a foot or anything. He uses a prosthesis."

"Seriously?"

She nodded sadly. "Owen doesn't hold it against Daniel, but my parents say Daniel's never really forgiven himself. He went off the deep end right after it happened. He got into drugs and stuff. He was pretty wild for a few years. My mom cried all the time. My parents were scared he was trying to kill himself. That's why Uncle Gray started training him with martial arts and stuff. He's fine now. He's stable and he doesn't drink or do drugs or anything, but he also doesn't really let go and have fun like he did when we were kids. I think he feels too guilty for that. He'll say the accident has nothing to do with it, but we all know it does. He hasn't been the same since then. I know he wishes he could trade places with Owen. I think, in the back of his mind, he thinks Owen won't be able to find a girlfriend or wife with his leg the way it is, so Daniel doesn't date girls. He didn't even go to the high school prom or anything. I heard our mom say he unintentionally tries to punish himself."

I thought of Daniel. I thought of his physical appearance and marveled at how crazy it was someone who looked like him and could probably have any girl he wanted refused to date. I quietly contemplated everything Ivy had just said, feeling like my heart was broken for him.

"I shouldn't have told you all that," she said, seeing me go introspective. "He would kill me if he knew I told you. I don't want you to judge him because of what I said. He really is a great person. That was a long time ago."

"I'm really glad you told me that," I said. "I was trying to get him to laugh all day today, and he just kept being so serious. I thought maybe he didn't like me or something."

"No, he really likes you. He told me before I came over here that he thought you were cool."

"Then why is he getting someone else to fill in for Trevor? Why doesn't he just stay with me until Trevor gets better?"

Ivy shrugged. "I don't know," she said. "You'll have to ask him that. But I think it's because he doesn't normally work with clients. Usually he stays home at the training center in Memphis."

Chapter 4

It was one o'clock in the morning when I kicked everyone out of my room so I could get some sleep. We always made sure to reserve multi-bedroom suites so that Denise and Trevor could have their own bedrooms. Denise was tired and went into her room right after we finished the show. It was quiet in the suite once everybody left, but I was still so amped from the show that it took me a while to fall asleep.

My eyes opened at 3am.

I was sweating and out of breath, and my heart was racing like mad in spite of the fact that I was laying in bed. A wave of nausea hit me as I focused on the clock, realizing I had only been asleep for an hour. I laid my head on the pillow and stared at the ceiling, begging myself to calm down and go back to sleep.

I threw the covers off. I was hot and sweaty and breathing heavily. It wasn't the first time I had experienced this—waking up in the middle of an anxiety attack or whatever it was. It was something that happened to me on a somewhat regular basis—and it definitely became more frequent while I was on tour. Sometimes I was able to make myself calm down and go back to sleep within a few minutes, and other times it would take me an hour or two.

I took deep breaths in and then out as I stared at the ceiling. I tried to convince myself that I wasn't dying and this was something that had happened a hundred times before. I did my best to get my nerves under control, but in moments like this, my brain seemed to overthink without my permission.

Tonight my thoughts turned to Daniel.

I thought about his brother and imagined the accident. I could see it in my mind's eye. I felt pain in my heart for Daniel and for his little brother and wanted to somehow comfort them both. Thinking about Daniel made me mad that he was planning on leaving me the following day. I had truly done my best to be nice to him, and I thought for sure he would fill in until Trevor got better.

As I lay there, I found myself wishing that Daniel would just take Trevor's place for good, and that's when I knew I was being irrational. I rolled over in an effort to comfort my aching stomach and distract myself from the ridiculous thoughts.

I stayed there for about half an hour, trying my best not to think of Daniel or any other stressful subjects before I finally broke down and reached out to him. If I needed company so bad, I probably should have just asked Denise to come crawl into bed with me. It was something I had done several times in the past, and she never gave me grief about it.

I didn't text Denise, though.

It was Daniel that I contacted.

I typed out a text to the number Denise had given me earlier.

Me: "Can you come to my room?"

Not even a minute had passed when I heard him come into the main door of the suite. I saw a light come on in the living room, and I squinted even though barely any of it was filtering into my bedroom.

Seconds later, my bedroom door opened and Daniel switched on the light. I closed my eyes and put my hand over my face, feeling shocked by the sudden brightness.

"Courtney?" He was speaking quietly, but his deep voice cut through the silent room.

"I'm fine," I assured him. "Can you please turn off the light?"

He turned off the light and started to cross to my bedside. "Can you turn off the living room light, too, so we don't wake Denise up?"

Daniel disappeared into the other room, turning off the light before coming to stand in my doorway again. There was still some light in the living room, and my eyes were already adjusted to the darkness, so I could see him standing there. He had on sweatpants and a fitted white t-shirt.

"Are you okay?" he asked.

"Yes."

He stood there as if waiting for me to explain why I had beckoned him.

"I just woke up feeling really anxious, and I wanted you to come in here."

My voice came out vulnerably, and this caused Daniel to walk toward me, stopping at my bedside. I scooted over and patted the bed, inviting him to sit down. In one motion, he took something from his backside, and set it securely on the bedside table as he sat on the edge of the bed.

"You brought a gun?" I asked.

"I wasn't planning on using it, but I figured I should have it just in case. I didn't know why you called."

He shifted and stared down at me. He was right next to me, and it still didn't feel close enough. I wanted to touch him—just reach out and rub his back or something crazy like that.

"Can you please just stay in here for a minute?" I asked. "Just lay here on top of the covers while I try to fall back asleep?"

"Is that what Trevor does?"

"No," I said defensively. "I mean I guess he has a couple of times, but nothing happens between us. The way you asked it makes me feel like you think I'm..." I hesitated. "I just wanted you to lay in here with me for a minute, that's all."

Daniel turned and stretched out onto the edge of my bed. I knew by the way he conducted himself that he thought it was his professional duty to do what I asked. Honestly, I really didn't care what compelled him to stay, I only cared that he was staying. He propped himself on the very edge of my bed, stiffly resting his head on the pillow.

I took a long, shaky breath.

"Are you okay?" he asked.

"Super nauseous," I whispered. "And cold sweats. I wake up like this sometimes—mostly when I'm on tour. It's a stomach ulcer that acts up when I'm on the road. Basically, I've been having a pending stomachache for the past seven years."

"I know the feeling," he said.

"You have pending stomachaches, too?"

"Yes," he said with no hesitation whatsoever. "All the time. I started putting a drop of peppermint oil in my water a few years ago, and that helps a little."

"Why do you get stomachaches?" I asked.

"Why do you?"

"Because I hate touring. I love my fans and everything, but touring tears me up physically. It's not just the bodily strain of being on the road, either. I just don't think I handle the pressure very well."

"Yes you do," he said. "Not many people could do what you do."

We stayed there in silence for what must have been at least two minutes before I spoke again.

"Why are you leaving," I asked.

"I'm not," he answered, thinking I was referring to leaving the bed.

"Why are you leaving the tour? Why are you going back to Memphis? Your sister told me you were leaving."

Daniel took a deep breath. "I talked to Gray earlier this evening. We've got a great guy lined up for you. Eric. He'll be here tomorrow, and I'll give him the rundown on everything before I head home."

"Why can't you do it?" I asked.

He was quiet for a moment as if contemplating how to answer my question. "It's like you said. I'm just not cut out for life on the road."

"It seems like you are doing a good job to me," I said, still resting my head on the pillow next to him.

"Well, thank you, but I'm better suited to work at the training center. I'm not really cut out for reassuring people and laughing at their jokes."

"You laughed at a couple of my jokes," I said.

"Only the ones that were funny," he said.

I thought back to our interactions during the course of the day. We had lots of time together while I was running around Miami doing interviews. We had several lengthy conversations, but I always felt like I had to drag information out of him. Ivy was right. He was a man of few words, and I could understand how some people might be offended by that. I thought about what she had told me and wondered how much of his quiet personality was a result of the accident.

I liked him so much. Truly identified with him and felt desperate to make him stay.

"I don't want a substitute. I want you to stay with me. I want you to come to New Orleans with us."

"I am a substitute," he said. "Anybody but Trevor is a substitute. You'll like Eric better than me, I promise."

"No, I won't. I don't want anyone else. I'll pay more if I have to."

Daniel breathed a little laugh. I was so close to him that I could feel his chest shake. I picked up my head and looked at him. There was enough light in the room that I could clearly see his face.

"I'm serious," I said, staring straight at him. "I'll pay whatever it takes to make you stay. I don't want you to leave."

He stared at me as if wondering if he could possibly be hearing me right. "You'll really like Eric," he said. "He's a good looking guy. Smart too. He was an Army Ranger. I have a picture of him on my phone if you want to see what he looks like."

"Why do you think I'll care what he looks like? Do you think I'm attracted to you or something?" I probably sounded a little offended because the truth was, I was.

"No," he said. "I'm just saying, you'll really like Eric. He's a good guy."

"I don't want Eric, though. I want you, Daniel."

He rubbed my shoulder in a comforting manner. "You just need to get some sleep," he said.

It sounded like he thought I was delirious, which was frustrating.

"Can you just think about staying, please?"

"Would it make you feel better if I say I'll think about it?" he asked.

"It will if you'll really think about it."

"Okay, I'll think about it, then," he said.

I knew he was just saying that to get me to quit asking. "I love your little sister," I said. "She's a sweetheart, and so cute."

"I really appreciate you being so nice to her. She loves your music and was really excited when I got the call to come down here."

"Let her come with us to New Orleans, then."

"No," he said instantly. "Even if I would decide to fill in for Trevor, there's no way I would take her. It's too much for me to try to protect both of you at the same time. That's out of the question. I can't even believe I let her talk me into coming here."

"It worked out fine," I said. "Nina and Jack loved her, and I think she helped them out backstage."

"Yeah, but it's not gonna happen again. I had to double up on peppermint oil worrying about both of you."

I let out a little laugh at his statement, figuring it was probably the truth. "Do you really have stomach problems?" I asked sincerely.

"Yes, I do."

"Me too."

"I'm sorry," he said.

"I'm sorry for you, too."

"It's fine," he said. "You learn to ignore it after about ten years."

"What in the world gave you a stomachache for that long, Daniel?"

"Nothing," he said. "I think you need to get some sleep."

"Why won't you talk to me?"

"I have been talking to you. I've been talking to you way more than I talk to most people."

"Please don't leave me," I whispered.

He rubbed my arm but didn't say anything.

"Please," I said, feeling like it was necessary to make him promise before I could possibly fall asleep.

"I really think you'll like Eric," he said. "How about we just let you meet him tomorrow, and we'll see how it goes from there?"

"And what if I meet him and say I still want you to stay? Will you stay?"

"Sure," he said.

I knew it wasn't an empty promise, but I also knew he was convinced I would like Eric.

"So if I still feel the same way tomorrow, you'll stay with me?"

"Yes," he said. "Until Trevor gets better."

That was a good enough for me. I smiled peacefully, feeling safe and secure and anxiety free for a change.

Chapter 5

It was just after 7am when I opened my eyes again. I was facing the clock on the bedside table, and it registered right away that I only had a few hours sleep. I almost began moving around and stretching out, but then I realized that I was still curled up next to Daniel, so rather than moving or adjusting, I stayed completely still.

I was overjoyed that he made the choice to stay in my room, and I didn't want to ruin it by doing something silly like waking up. Daniel was still on top of the covers. He was sleeping stiffly on the edge of the bed, and I knew any sudden movement would wake him up. So, for a few minutes, I stayed completely still.

Maybe it was ridiculous since I was just getting to know Daniel Bishop, but I had never felt so safe in my whole life, and I wanted to stay right there curled up next to him forever. Being next to him was like medicine, and I just rested there, contently basking in the sweet relief I felt.

Was it possible to fall in love with someone this quickly?

I had a whole string of thoughts about love at first sight and the impossibility of it as I lay there, trying to remain completely motionless. I wanted to stretch out, but I didn't want the moment to end.

I'd never felt this way about anyone.

I couldn't stop thinking that it must be love.

I loved his story.

I even thought I loved his family despite the fact that I had never met them.

Somewhere deep in my bones, I just innately loved Daniel Bishop for who he was. I thought about the accident with his brother and the baggage he had been carrying for so long, and I realized that none of that was a surprise to me—it was like I already knew him and somehow already had his story etched in my heart before his sister even shared it with me.

He was a breathtakingly handsome man. His face was like a chiseled superhero and his body looked and moved like he was an athlete, but my attraction to him had little to do with his physical appearance. It was more than that. It was like my heart found its home when I was next to him.

I was overwhelmed with love and emotion as I lay there. I couldn't see his face from my current position. All I could see without moving was his chest, chin, and neck. I marveled at the way his dark facial hair grew in patches along his jaw, and I found that it was nearly impossible to keep myself from kissing his skin. There was a glorious indention on the side of his neck, and I focused on it, realizing I could literally see his pulse. It was subtle, but I noticed the tiny jumping motion of his heart beating steadily.

I was so caught up with love or desire or some mixture of the two that I did the unthinkable. I slowly moved forward and let my lips gently fall on his neck, right at the spot where I could see his heart beating. I felt the short stubble of his facial hair against my lips, and I knew beyond the shadow of a doubt that I never wanted to kiss another man.

My heart wanted to explode.

My lips were open just slightly when they fell on his skin, and a crashing wave of love and desire washed over me when I realized I could taste him.

Heaven. That was the only way I could possibly describe how it felt—like I must have died and gone to Heaven. All was right with the world in that moment when my lips were on Daniel Bishop.

Then suddenly, he began to move.

In one quick motion he sat up, swiveling around and letting his feet hit the ground. Just like that, he was sitting at the edge of the bed with his back toward me. I watched him stretch, the muscles of his back creating ridges that were visible through the thin white T-shirt. It was all I could do to stop myself from reaching out to touch him. He turned to focus on me and smiled when he saw my eyes were barely open.

"Good morning, Ms. Cole."

My heart fell at the sound of him calling me by my last name. I gave him a little smile, but it was forced. "Morning," I said sleepily.

"Sorry to wake you," he said. "I think you might have been dreaming."

I wanted to insist that I had not been dreaming, but instead I just gave him another fake, sleepy smile.

"I should probably be getting back to my room to check on Ivy. Denise is up. She's right out here in the living room, but if you need me for anything, just call."

I gave him a thankful nod. "Thank you for staying in here," I said. "I know you didn't have to do that."

He smiled. "My pleasure."

He turned and started to stand up, but before he could, I instinctually reached out and grabbed his shirt. This made him turn around and look at me again.

I was about to say, "I wasn't dreaming when I kissed you," but I was so stunned by his gorgeous dark-featured face when he turned that I couldn't get the words to come out of my mouth. I stared at him, feeling too speechless to think of what to say. "Uh, what'd you decide?" I asked.

"About what?"

"About New Orleans."

"I'll bring Eric over in a little bit," he said. "You can let me know how you're feeling after you meet him."

I almost said I already knew how I'd feel, but instead I just smiled and nodded, letting him know I was satisfied with that answer.

He stared at me for a few seconds and I thought he was about to standup, but instead he reached out and put his hand on my head. I knew enough about Daniel to know this type of maneuver was completely out of character for him, but he could probably tell that I was aching for his affection, and he went out of his comfort zone to give it to me.

"Are you feeling better?" he asked sweetly.

I nodded with a tiny reassuring grin.

"Good," he said with a contemplative smile. "I'm glad. Maybe you can get some more rest."

And just like that, he stood up, tucking the gun that was on the bedside into the waistline of his pants before heading for the door. I saw him interact with Denise for a moment, but I couldn't hear what they were saying.

I stayed in bed for half an hour or so, thinking about Daniel and Trevor and the fact that I only had two more shows to go. I had a lot of things on my mind, but I was so exhausted that sleep found me again.

The next thing I knew, I was being woken up. I felt someone rubbing my arm, and I opened my eyes to find Denise sitting on the edge of my bed, smiling down at me.

"Good morning, sleepy bones," she said.

"Morning. What time is it?"

I could've easily glanced at the clock, but I just let her tell me.

"It's ten-thirty. I would've let you sleep, but Daniel is here with Trevor's new replacement, and he seems to think you would want to talk to him personally before he heads out."

I sat straight up. "Before who heads out?"

"Daniel and his sister. I think they need to go ahead and leave for the airport. She's so cute. She was out at the beach this morning in her gymnastics leotard."

I stood up, sliding clumsily into my fluffy white slippers. There was a matching white robe draped over the foot of my bed, and I shrugged into it. I absolutely never popped out of bed that quickly, and Denise glanced at me like she was surprised I was in such a hurry.

"I told him not to leave," I said.

"That's why he's here," she whispered, nodding.

I headed into the living room, still feeling stiff, sleepy, and out-of-it. I didn't even care that I looked like a mess; all I cared about was catching Daniel before he left.

The two men were sitting on the couch, and they both stood up when I came into the room.

When it came to stature, they looked like they could have been twins. Their facial features were different, but they were both tall, confident, athletic-looking men with broad shoulders and dark hair. I thought of Trevor and how he would fit this same description, and I wondered if Alpha Security only hired this specific type of man.

I glanced back and forth between the two of them, realizing that they were both smiling at me. "I apologize for waking you, Ms. Cole," Daniel said.

"Courtney," I said, looking straight at Daniel. "And I'm glad you did."

"I wanted you to meet Eric Matthews," he continued.

I came to stand near the gentleman, smiling as I extended a hand to shake Eric's.

"It's very nice to meet you," Eric said.

"You too," I agreed.

Daniel was right. I could see how he would have assumed that I would like Eric just as much as I liked him or Trevor. Physically, the three men could've almost been interchangeable. Eric's hair was slightly lighter and a little longer, but he had a handsome, inviting smile, and by everyone else's standards, I should have liked Eric just as much as Daniel. The problem was, Eric wasn't Daniel.

"Eric's been with us for about a year," Daniel said. "And he had experience with the Secret Service before that, so I promise, you're in good hands."

I wanted to be in no one's hands but Daniel's, and my gut clinched at the way he made things sound so final. He must have thought I was delirious when I asked him to stay last night.

Denise walked across the living room and sat at the table, staring at her laptop and not paying any attention to us. During the next few seconds, I fought an internal battle. I could see that the wheels were set in motion for Eric to take Daniel's place. I knew that Daniel wasn't comfortable with life on the road, and I begged myself to just chill and stop being so selfish and go with the flow. I told myself that obviously Daniel did not *want* to be here with me, or he wouldn't be so adamant about leaving.

I knew I should let Eric take over.

I knew I should forget about Daniel Bishop.

But in spite of knowing those things, I still looked straight at Daniel and said, "I thought you were just going to work for me until Trevor got back."

I glanced at Eric and saw that his smile faded a little at my statement.

"No offense," I said. "I'm sure you're really good. But I was under the impression that Daniel was doing the job. We already talked about it."

I looked at Daniel who remained expressionless. I watched his chest rise and fall as he took a deep breath.

"I think Daniel and his sister need to get to the airport," Denise interjected without looking up from her work at the table.

I tried not to be frustrated with her because she had no idea how important this was to me. "Thanks," I called sarcastically.

I turned to focus on Daniel, feeling only slightly ashamed of myself for not being able to hide my annoyance.

"Can I talk to you in here for a second?" I asked, pointing toward my bedroom with a thumb over my shoulder.

"Sure," he said, following me.

Maybe it was silly or selfish of me to feel this way, but I was so angry and torn up over the idea of Daniel leaving that silent tears began streaming down my face. I didn't want to be emotional about it, there was nothing I could do to stop the tears. Denise had opened the curtains in my bedroom, so it was light in there when we stepped inside. Daniel followed me in, and I made sure he was clear of the door before I closed it. I turned to face him and saw his expression change and soften when he noticed my tearstained cheeks.

"What's the matter?" he asked quietly.

"What do you think?" I asked incredulously.

"I'm sorry," he said. "I really thought you'd like Eric. His personality is a lot like Trevor's, and—"

I cut him off. "I already told you I wanted you to stay," I said, drying my cheeks with the sleeve of my robe. "I thought you agreed to do it."

"I did, and I still will if you want, I just thought that after you met Eric, you'd see that—"

"See what? That you're both capable of protecting me from bad guys?"

"Yes, and he's funny and nice, too."

"So are you."

Daniel tilted his head with a slightly skeptical expression. "I'm just saying... he's got a lot more experience in the field."

"I don't care about training. I said I wanted you to stay, and you promised me you would. Are you going back on your promise?"

"No."

"Then why is he here?"

"Because I thought once you met him you would—"

"I don't. I met him, and I don't want him to stay. I'm sure he's great. I know he's probably a wonderful security guard, but I don't want him. I want you. You promised you would stay if I wanted you to, and that's what I want."

Daniel took a deep breath, looking at me like he was about to say something and then changed his mind. "Okay," he said simply.

"Okay?" I asked.

He nodded.

"I'm sorry that we made him come down here for nothing. I already knew that I—"

"That's fine," he said. "We took him off a job to bring him over here, so they'll be glad to have him back."

"Thank you," I said. "And please tell Eric it has nothing to do with him. I'm just already so torn up over Trevor, and all the switching around was making me a little..." I hesitated, touching my stomach and hoping this vague explanation was enough to explain my tears.

"I understand," Daniel said. "It's no problem. I'll take care of it." He sighed, contemplating whether or not we had addressed everything that needed to be addressed. "I know you've got the day off today," he said. "Denise mentioned you wanting to go to the beach."

I nodded.

"Would it be all right if I let Eric cover for a few hours while I take care of getting Ivy on her plane?"

I nodded again. "But she's welcome to stay."

He shook his head. "Thanks, but I need to get her back home. I'm not even gonna tell her you offered because she'd hate me for saying 'no'. I'll be back this afternoon. In the meantime, Eric will take you wherever you want to go."

"Thank you," I said.

He gave me a little smile. "I'm happy to do it," he said sweetly.

I figured there was a possibility he was just saying that to be nice, but I really didn't care as long as he was staying.

"I'll fill Eric in on what's going on. He'll be waiting out there whenever you're ready to go."

Chapter 6

I spent the next hour washing my hair and getting ready to go out. Jake was already on his way to New Orleans, but he had left several outfits in my closet, all of which were appropriate for a day at the beach. I had to smile when I saw a note on one of the swimsuits that said, "Please wear this one." He and Nina were on the road with the rest of the crew, but my bus wasn't scheduled to leave until that evening after dinner.

I put on the swimsuit Jake had recommended, and over it, I wore a long, flowy dress. I added a hat and oversized sunglasses, not only because they helped me escape photographers, but also because I liked how they looked with the dress.

I had been to Miami several times before, and I always went to the same stretch of beach. There was good shopping and restaurants nearby, and I never got hassled. Denise and Vick would both be riding on the bus with me to New Orleans, and they were excited to enjoy a day off as well.

The two of them, along with Eric, were waiting in the living room for me when I finished getting dressed, and we got on the road right away. Denise wanted to do some shopping, so Vick went with her while Eric and I went to the beach. I attracted a couple of photographers, but it was an upscale section of the city, and for the most part, they kept their distance and remained respectful. I came really close to taking off my dress since I had Jake's recommended swimsuit underneath, but I considered what Daniel said about my gold stage outfit, and I opted to leave it on.

Eric and I stayed at the beach for about an hour. We did some people watching and soaking in the sun before the other two came back and asked us if we wanted to grab some lunch.

Eric was everything Daniel promised he would be. He was smart, funny, considerate, and extremely easy to get along with. He was such a gentleman— the perfect bodyguard and companion—the perfect replacement for Trevor. But never once during my time with Eric did I regret asking Daniel to come back. In fact, I couldn't wait for him to return.

After lunch, we went back to the hotel. My suite came with access to a rooftop pool, and since I hadn't used it at all during my stay, I decided to go out there. Eric came with me, but Vick and Denise both decided to lay low in their respective rooms. We were all accustomed to giving each other space. It was something you got good at when you spent so much time on the road together.

Eric and I had only been poolside for a little while when he got a text from Daniel saying that he had been delayed by stopping at the store to pick up some clothes and supplies for the trip, but that he was on his way.

I got nervous at the thought of Daniel showing up while we were at the pool, and I actually wondered what I could be doing when he arrived that would get his attention. *Should I be swimming in the pool, or would he like it better if I was stretched out in a lounge chair, reading a book?* I had to laugh at myself for thinking such absurd thoughts. I had never in my life wanted so badly to impress a man.

Eric and I had been in and out of the pool, but we were both standing in the shallow end with our backs against the wall when Daniel arrived. I watched him as he stepped outside taking in his surroundings.

He had changed clothes since the last time I saw him. He had on khaki slacks and a light colored, short-sleeve shirt. His skin was tanned, his haircut was sharp, and he had on stylish sunglasses. He looked like Miami's most eligible bachelor. I was trying my best to contain a huge grin at the sight of him when I noticed his serious expression.

Eric hopped out of the pool without using the stairs. His sudden movement made a splash that caused me to shift to the side and stare up at him. Water ran off of his perfect male body, and I realized I didn't even care. He was extremely attractive, and yet he might as well if been my brother with how indifferent I felt toward him.

"Hey boss," Eric said.

"Hey," Daniel returned, looking at him and then at me. "Where's Vick?" Daniel asked. "Is it just you two up here?"

"Yep," Eric said, grabbing a towel and beginning to dry off. "We went to the beach earlier, but Court didn't get to swim, so she wanted to come up here."

Daniel looked at me. He was standing up, and I was way down in the pool, so I had to really tilt my head to see him. It was bright, and I squinted into the sun. Daniel's expression remained serious, and my heart sped up as I wondered what he was thinking. I so badly wanted him to like me that his stoicism caused a yearning sensation in my chest.

"We ate the best fish tacos I've ever had," Eric said, trying to make pleasant conversation about our day. "I might have to fly back to Miami just to eat them again."

Daniel didn't comment on the tacos. He came to stand a little closer to me, still looking like he was accessing the situation. I couldn't stand it any longer; I had to try to get his attention. I swam to the steps and slowly got out of the pool, doing my best to walk gracefully like a model without looking like I was trying too hard. Jake really knew what he was doing as a stylist, and I wanted so badly for Daniel to take a second to look at my swimsuit, but he barely glanced at me. I hardly had the chance to get my feet onto dry land when he picked up a towel and wrapped it around me.

"No thanks," I said, feeling stubborn and handing the towel back to him. "I wanted to get a little sun while we're out here. I didn't get to lay out at the beach."

Daniel's expression remained serious. "If you don't mind, Ms. Cole, Eric and I will talk for a few minutes so he can be on his way."

"Not at all," I said. I reached out to give Eric a sideways hug. "Thank you," I said. "I had fun today."

"Me too," he said sweetly. "And next time, I'm not taking it easy on you." (He was talking about the swimming race we had down and back the length of the pool. I was a good swimmer, but I knew he had let me win.)

I smiled and stuck my tongue out at him.

"Okay, so, we're gonna sit right over here and finish up," Daniel said, pointing to the nearby table as if he wanted Eric to take a seat in one of the chairs.

"That's fine," I said casually. "I'm just going to read."

My hat and sunglasses were sitting on a table, and I put them both on before stretching out on a lounge chair. I had already applied SPF 50 sunblock, so I was relatively sure I wasn't getting a tan, but it felt good to stretch out and relax next to the pool nonetheless. I had a few books downloaded onto my phone, and I scrolled to the one I had been meaning to start reading.

Daniel and Eric talked for the next fifteen minutes while I read the first chapter of the book. I was a little bit preoccupied with thoughts of Daniel, but the book was enjoyable, which thankfully helped me ignore him while they had their conversation.

"Bye Court," Eric said once they had finished. "It was great meeting you."

"You too!" I said, waving at him.

I watched as he walked through the door, disappearing behind the mirrored glass. I glanced at Daniel who was now standing a few feet away, looking down at me.

"I like your sunglasses," I said.

"Thanks."

"Did you get Ivy off to Memphis?"

He nodded and glanced at this watch. "She should actually be home soon. It's only like a two-and-a-half hour flight."

"Thank you for staying," I said.

"Seems like you were getting along just fine with Eric."

Daniel was a true professional, but he was slightly annoyed, which delighted me way more than it should have.

"We got along great," I said, pushing his buttons. "We had a really fun day."

"Are you trying to tell me you wish he was staying?"

"No."

"Because I can make that happen if that's what you want."

"I just said I didn't."

"Then stop telling me how much fun you two had. I already had to hear enough of that from Eric just now. He didn't even want to go back to his other job."

I smirked at him for making such a statement, but I was secretly elated.

"Is this what you wore to the beach?" he asked gesturing at me.

My heart was beating a thousand miles an hour as he looked me over.

"Yes, but I had a dress over it."

"Good."

"Why? Don't you like it? I thought it was really Miami-ish. Jake specifically told me to wear this one."

"Why would you want a man picking out your clothes? He's just going to give you stuff like this that barely covers anything."

"I think it covers plenty," I said glancing down at myself. "You should've seen some of those girls at the beach today. I felt like a nun leaving my dress on."

"Great," he said seriously. "You should always feel like a nun. Nuns are the best. You should think of becoming a nun."

I wanted so badly to get a rise out of him that my chest began buzzing at the thought that this conversation was causing his temper to flare. I reached out and took hold the lounge chair that was next to me, pulling it closer and patting it as if indicating he should sit down.

"Tell me something," I said, stashing my phone next to me on the table.

"Like what?"

"Talk to me about your family. You said you have other siblings besides Ivy. Tell me about them. Tell me about your parents. Tell me what you like to eat for a midnight snack."

"I don't eat midnight snacks," he said as he sat down.

"Then tell me about your family."

"I'm the oldest," he said.

"I've got two younger brothers—Owen and Wesley—we call him Wes. Ivy's the youngest."

"Is everyone in Memphis?"

"All but Wes. He's in college in London."

"England?"

He nodded. "He's always wanted to go over there ever since we were kids. He likes the accent."

"What about your parents?"

"My mom and dad both work for the family business. My mom's name is Rose. She does advertising and accounting and stuff, and my dad, Jesse, runs the whole operation with my grandpa. They're not just behind a desk, though. They both still build bikes. I don't think they'll ever get out of the garage, no matter how big the business gets."

"That's cool," I said. "I've always wanted to learn how to drive a motorcycle."

"Yeah, they're fun," he said. "What about your family? You said you're an only child."

"Yep, it's just me. I started singing when I was really young. My mom moved us to California when I was eight so that I could audition for stuff. I did a few commercials and some work as an extra on Nickelodeon and Disney before I got a record deal. Mom traveled around with me for a while when I first started touring, but she's happier staying home with my stepdad. It's better for both of us. We get along, but we don't talk everyday or anything. She's kind of a hippie-artist type—lost in her own head."

"Does she still live in California?" he asked.

I nodded.

"Is that where you're gonna settle eventually?"

"I guess. I have a house there and friends. That's where I stay when I'm not touring. It's the only real home I know."

I wanted him to take the hint and invite me to Memphis, but he just smiled at me thoughtfully.

"How's your stomach?" he asked.

"Better. I wasn't quite up for the fish tacos, but I did get down a few bites. They were pretty good."

"A few bites doesn't sound like enough," he said.

"Believe me, I'm used to it," I said, patting my midsection.

"I bought you some peppermint oil while I was out," he said. "You can't ingest just any of them, but while I was out, I tracked down a place that had a good brand, and got a bottle of it for you. Denise has it in your room. You just put a drop of it in your bottled water."

He was sitting on the edge of the lounge chair with his hands on his knees, and I reached out and put my hand on his. "Thank you so much," I said. "That was really thoughtful."

I felt him finch, and I thought he might take his hand out from under mine, but he left it there. "You're welcome," he said. "I hope it helps."

Chapter 7

Vick decided at the last minute to hop a flight from Miami to New Orleans, so Denise, Daniel, my driver, Anthony, and I were the only ones on the tour bus during our trip. We headed out at 8pm with plans to arrive in New Orleans before noon the following morning. Anthony was used to driving at night and had already caught up on his sleep before we left.

There was a little living room area in the front of the bus, and Denise sat in there, talking with Daniel and me for the first part of our trip. He was still a little guarded, but the more time we spent together, the more open he was. And the more I learned about him, the more smitten I was.

He told us about his great-grandfather—the man he was named after. He was a preacher before he retired, and Daniel's grandfather, Jacob, had taken over the church and was still the pastor there. He said his family got together for lunch every Sunday after church. He told me about his Nana's southern cooking and laughed about how she had to double and triple her recipes over the years as the family had grown. I hadn't been raised going to church or doing big family get-togethers, and the way Daniel talked about it made me feel like I might have missed out on something.

We spoke for about four hours—talking about our childhoods and growing up, but Daniel never mentioned the accident. Having no idea that I had completely fallen for Daniel, Denise stayed in the living room area with us, talking and sharing her own experiences. She seemed to be enjoying the conversation as much as I was.

It was almost midnight when Anthony stopped for one of his rare breaks. He pulled into a truck stop to gas up and use the restroom, and I glanced at my phone, realizing how late it was. "I'm tired," I said.

"Me too," Denise agreed. "I planned on going to bed early tonight, but we got to talking." She stood up to stretch, and I smiled at Daniel.

"Trevor's got a bunk in the back," I said.

He gave me a little shake of the head. "I was planning on staying up here with Anthony," he said. He patted the couch. "I'll probably just stretch out right here."

"Night," Denise said, heading to the back of the bus.

"Night," I called before focusing on Daniel again.

I felt nervous now that we were alone.

"It's kinda like camping," I said with a gesture to our surroundings. "Do you ever go camping?"

"Nana and Pa have a cabin up in Dyersburg. My parents and aunt and uncle helped them remodel it a few years ago, so it's not really roughing it, but it is out on a lake, so you feel like you're camping."

"Will you take me sometime?" I asked. "Dyersburg sounds kinda dangerous, but I'd still like to go see your family's cabin."

He let out a little laugh. "Dyersburg isn't dangerous at all, and the cabin's really not in that town, anyway. It's just close to there."

"Is it in Tennessee?" I asked.

He nodded. "About an hour or two north of Memphis."

"Will you take me sometime?"

"Sure," he said.

"Sure as in you're just saying that to be nice, or sure like you'll actually take me?"

"Both, I guess," he said with a little smile and shrug. "I'm not really sure how many gigs you play in Memphis."

"I've played there before," I said. "But it's been a long time." I felt the uncontrollable urge to touch him, so I reached out and pinched his leg. "I don't have to be playing a gig in Memphis to go there, though."

He smiled at me. "I guess you're right."

"So, are you inviting me?" I asked. *So what if I sounded desperate.* I didn't even care. I was desperate.

"Definitely," he said.

"Can I come train at Alpha?"

During our conversation on the bus, Daniel had told us more about the day-to-day operations at Alpha Security. I was aware that it was a good company, otherwise I wouldn't have hired them to begin with, but the details he shared with me made me want to go there and see it for myself. Maybe I just wanted to go there to see Daniel. Either way, I wanted to go.

"You wouldn't be the only female training there," he said. "We have a woman working for us named Kara Harding. She's an Olympic silver medalist in Judo."

"Trevor told me about Judo," I said. "He demonstrated one of the moves on Jake," I added, laughing at the memory. "I think Jake was sore for a week. He does Jiu-Jitsu, too—like they do in cage fighting. I hear him talking about it."

"I know," Daniel said. "All of our guys do it."

"He said you make him go to the gym while we're on the road."

"We do," Daniel said. "Gray requires the guys to do six hours a week of training while they're in the field so they stay in shape."

I smiled. "That's what Trevor said. He gets all excited when we go to a city that has a big gym. Denise gives him a hard time about it. She says he just claims it's mandatory so that he has an excuse to get away from us."

"No, it is mandatory," Daniel said. "We make sure the guys stay active in their training."

"He's got a pull-up bar in the back of the bus," I said, gesturing with a thumb over my shoulder in that direction.

"Good man," Daniel said. "Has he taught you anything?"

I shook my head. "After I saw him do that move on Jake, I was like 'no, thank you'."

"I'm not talking about Judo. I'm talking about basic, self-defense stuff. Has he shown you any of that?"

I shook my head again. "That's what I have him for."

"Yeah, but he's not with you twenty-four hours a day." He gestured around us. "He's not with you right now. What if I was a bad guy and I were to try to overtake you right now. Would you know what to do?"

I smiled inwardly, wishing he would try to overtake me, but I didn't say that. "I could gouge your eyes out," I said.

"Yeah, that would hurt," Daniel said. "But you really should know a basic cross-choke, at least. That's something you can do from a vulnerable position like on your back."

"What's a cross-choke?" I asked.

"It's where you take a hold of your attacker's lapel or shirt collar and use it as leverage to choke them."

Daniel demonstrated by making an "X" with his arms in the air in front of him. He flexed his fists and pulled downward just slightly as if this little motion should explain everything. I stared at him like I was totally confused, and he let out a little laugh.

"Look," he said. "I'll let you try it on me."

We were both sitting on the couch that lined the wall in my bus. I was sitting cross-legged, and Daniel shifted and leaned over me so that we were face-to-face. He was only about a foot or two away. It was the, *I'm about to kiss you* position, and I felt completely overwhelmed. I took an unsteady breath, begging myself internally to remain calm.

"I'm not going to hurt you," he said.

"I'm not scared," I said.

"Why are you struggling to catch your breath?"

He was right. His proximity left me totally overwhelmed. My chest was rising and falling rapid breaths, and there was nothing I could do to make myself calm down.

"I'm just nervous about learning something new," I said, lying.

"Don't be nervous," he said, staring at me sweetly. He took my right hand and put it into the left collar of his shirt where the backside of my hand was against his neck. "Take a hold of my collar," he said. "Don't be scared. You're not going to hurt anything. Reach your hand way back there and hold it tight."

I did what he told me to do, feeling crazy with anticipation as the back of my hand rubbed against his neck.

"Now do the same thing with the other hand," he said.

I put my left hand into the right side of his collar.

"Go deeper," he said. "You really have to get way back there so that you have enough leverage."

I inched my hands further back into his collar. "I'm gonna stretch out your shirt," I said.

"Don't worry about my shirt. If I was attacking you right now, you wouldn't care about my shirt."

I kept a hold of his collar with the backs of my hands resting on his neck and my arms in that crossed position he showed me.

"Now hold on tight to my collar and move your arms so that your elbows are moving outward."

I moved slowly, but I felt the shirt tightening around his neck, cinching up like a tourniquet. "Wow!" I said. "So, I'm choking you with your own shirt? Is that the idea?"

"Yes," he said. "Really, it's this bone right here that's supposed to be cutting off the circulation, but you use my shirt for leverage." He touched the spot on his neck where my wrist bone came into contact with his artery. He shifted my arm so that it was positioned a little differently. "The deeper you go when you grab my shirt, the better. It's gonna make your arm bone hit my neck in just the right spot and cut off circulation when you tighten it. Now, keep a hold of my collar and squeeze tightly with your elbows going out to the side... yesssss," he said in a breathless way that let me know I was succeeding at choking him.

I let go instantly and smiled at him with wide eyes feeling so proud of myself that I had learned something.

"Did I really just choke you?"

"Yes," he said.

"Did I hurt your shirt?"

"No, but it wouldn't matter if you did. If somebody's attacking you, you're not going to care about hurting their shirt."

He sat down next to me, and I felt disappointed that he had moved. "Can I try it again?" I asked. It wasn't only that I wanted him hovering over me (although that was a bonus). I actually enjoyed learning the move and thought it was pretty practical.

Daniel smiled and moved to hover over me again.

"Okay, so this hand goes in this side, and this one goes right here," I said, talking myself through it.

"Yep."

"The deeper the better," I added, shimmying my hand along the sides of his neck till it felt like my fingers could almost touch each other.

"Yep."

"And then I hold onto your shirt while I pull my arms down like..."

"Yep," he said in that same hoarse, choking tone that made me laugh.

I loosened the grip I had on his collar, but I couldn't bear to let him go completely. He was so perfectly close to me that I dreaded the time when our lesson was over. I left my hands loosely in place as a confused look crossed my face.

"I guess it doesn't have to be a shirt," I said. "You could do it with a jacket or anything."

"Exactly," he said.

"What if the guy doesn't have a shirt on?"

"Well, I really hope that never happens, but if it does, I guess you could try your eye-gouging idea. Or a swift head-butt might work in a pinch."

"Or I could just have you with me to protect me."

"You could. I guess people who can hire me to be with them all the time don't really have to learn Jiu-Jitsu."

He pulled back just a little like he might leave his current position, but I tightened my grip on his collar.

"Daniel," I whispered. I watched in awe as he scanned my face. I could see that he began struggling to catch his breath just as I had been doing the whole time.

He smiled and shook his head, glancing away before looking at me again. "You're going to get me in all sorts of trouble, Courtney."

He shifted his head and then pulled back a little as if hinting that we should break contact, but I didn't let him go. He was still struggling to regulate his breathing as he glanced at the wall behind me.

"I think I should've never... I think I'm terrible at... I probably should have known better than to... That's why I shouldn't have come on this trip. It's just that you're a beautiful woman, and I, uh... I can't."

"You can't what?" I asked, gently tugging downward on his neck just a little to try to get him to look at me.

His eyes met mine. "I've never met anyone like you, Courtney. I'm afraid I'm having a little trouble maintaining professionalism here."

His words caused me to shiver. I loved the way his mouth moved when he spoke, and I loved the way he said my name. I wanted him to say it over and over.

He closed his eyes and let out a little sigh. "I shouldn't have put myself in this position. I'm actually relieved Trevor never showed you any Jiu-Jitsu. He didn't, did he?"

I smiled. "No, he didn't."

Daniel scanned my face again. I could tell he was having an internal battle as he regarded me, and I was so happy about it.

"Trevor and I never have trouble maintaining professionalism," I assured him.

"Thank God," he whispered.

"Even if he would've tried to show me this move, I would have just learned it and let him go. I wouldn't have held onto him like this."

"Good," he whispered, still staring at me.

We were remarkably close.

I bit my lip shyly. "Because things aren't the same with me and Trevor as they are with you and me," I said.

"Sorry that took so long!" Anthony said, startling both of us as he opened the bus door.

It was a good thing I let go of Daniel's collar because he stood up so quickly, I probably would have ripped his shirt had I held onto it.

Chapter 8

I went to my bunk in the back of the bus wondering how I could ever fall asleep after being so close to kissing Daniel and not succeeding.

I had tried to convince Daniel to sleep in Trevor's bunk, which was close to mine, but he insisted that he was comfortable on the couch. He said it was because he didn't want to intrude on Trevor's space, but I could tell he was trying to create a little distance. I had no idea whether it was because he was trying to be professional with me or if it had more to do with the guilt he carried about his brother. Part of me thought the latter was true, but I tried not to let that enter my thinking because I wasn't supposed to know about it in the first place.

I tried to go to sleep, but I couldn't stop thinking about him. I replayed parts of the conversation I had with him and Denise, and I caught myself smiling and repeating specific exchanges. He was a serious person, but I was already beginning to notice a change in his demeanor during the short time I had gotten to know him. I felt happy that he had loosened up a little around me, and I sincerely hoped it was because he liked me and not just because he was growing more comfortable in this situation.

I woke up the following morning at 9am with no stomachache whatsoever. This rarely happened while I was on tour, and I contributed it both to the peppermint oil and the person who gave it to me.

We made it to New Orleans before noon just like Anthony promised, and he dropped us off at our hotel, which was a lovely place near the French Quarter. I had played in New Orleans several times in the past, and I always stayed at the same place and had a great experience. I was especially happy about this one because I knew the suite had plenty of room for Daniel to have his own bedroom without feeling like he was taking over Trevor's space.

The concert was the following evening, and I had no media engagements (other than a phone interview) before then, so I had an entire day to do nothing but be a tourist and eat Cajun food.

"What are you going to do today?" Denise asked once we got settled in the room.

"I'll probably make Daniel take me around the French Quarter."

"Do you need me for anything?" she asked.

"No, why?"

"Gabe's cousin lives here," she said. "I was thinking about calling her."

I knew her boyfriend, Gabe, was from the south, but I didn't know exactly where. I nodded instantly. "You should call her," I said.

"Are you sure you don't need me?"

"Absolutely."

Daniel had been in his bedroom, but he came out as Denise and I were having this conversation. He had on jeans and a T-shirt with a lightweight hoodie, and I smiled at myself for noticing what he was wearing.

"Court just volunteered you to drag her around the French Quarter all day," Denise said.

Daniel smiled and shrugged. "That's why I'm here—to do as the lady wishes."

"Okay, well I'm going to go call Gabe's cousin, if you're sure."

"Definitely," I said. "Have fun. I'll be fine."

Denise smiled and took off toward her bedroom, and I focused on Daniel.

"Have you ever had gumbo?"

"Yeah, once."

"In New Orleans?"

"No, it was in Memphis."

"I'm pretty sure that doesn't count."

"Does it help if the person who made it was from Louisiana?"

I was actually jealous that someone had made him gumbo and I didn't even know who it was. It could've been some old man, and there I was, assuming it was a smoking hot 25-year-old lady.

"Who made you gumbo?" I asked, even though I begged myself not to care.

"One of the guys who came in to do a clinic at Alpha was from Louisiana—Lafayette, I think. He made a big pot of it for all of us." He lifted his eyebrows at me. "Is that authentic enough for you?"

I smiled. "I wasn't asking to test the authenticity."

"Why were you asking?" he asked.

There was no way I could say that I was jealous of the person who had theoretically cooked him food, so I just smiled and shrugged and pretended I didn't really know why I was asking.

I took a few minutes to get dressed. I put on skinny jeans with a graphic T-shirt that had a monkey holding a toy camera. I put my hair in a ponytail and pulled it through the back of a baseball cap before tying it into a bun. Then I clipped on a curly, brunette hairpiece that looked entirely real. I added fake glasses and my favorite pair of bubblegum pink Chuck Taylors, and I walked out of my bedroom, smiling at the sight of Daniel who was sitting on the couch, waiting for me. He stood up the second he saw me.

"You look so different," he said, checking me out. "Like a normal girl."

"That's because I am a normal girl."

"I mean, I don't think we're going to get hassled very much with you wearing that. You look really normal."

"Thanks," I said in a hesitant, sarcastic voice that said he wasn't really complimenting me.

"This is exactly why I don't work in the field," he said. "What I should've said was, you look gorgeous, Ms. Cole. Radiant."

"Please go back to calling me Courtney."

He stood and took a step toward me. "You look gorgeous, Courtney."

I stepped toward him slowly, squinting playfully at him like he was in trouble. "Oh, because I thought you just said I look *normal*."

"Normal was a terrible choice," he said. "You're anything but normal. All I meant was that people might not recognize you with that cap on."

"Now you're just trying to backpedal," I said, smiling.

The living room was huge and open, and he was standing there while I meandered closer and closer to him.

"I'm not backpedaling. You know what you look like. You don't need me to tell you how beautiful you are."

I came to stand right in front of him, staring into his dark eyes. "Yes I do," I said.

He regarded me with a serious expression. "You're beautiful." He said the words in a quiet tone as he glanced toward Denise's door, which was closed.

"What?" I asked, turning my ear toward him.

"You're the most beautiful woman I have ever seen in my whole life," he whispered sincerely.

This made me smile at him. "You didn't have to go that far," I said, teasing him.

I wanted so badly to take a hold of him and kiss him, but I knew I couldn't do it. Denise was in the next room, and besides, I feared I would push him away if I made a move like that.

"Ready?" I asked with a smile and shrug.

***

What followed was one of the best days of my entire life. I was fortunate in my career to have been all over the world, but this day spent in New Orleans, Louisiana perhaps topped them all.

Daniel and I spent the day enjoying each other's company, and we didn't force anything. It was late spring, and the weather was absolutely gorgeous. We took the day as it came, eating, shopping, and doing a whole lot of nothing.

At least ten people told me I looked like Courtney Cole, but I just laughed at them. I had never been able to get away with that before, even with the hairpiece. I attributed it to the fact that Daniel was behaving less like a bodyguard and more like my boyfriend (at least that's what I hoped).

There was a brass band playing in Jackson Square, and we sat on a bench and watched them for two hours straight. Tourists would walk up to them and dance or otherwise interact for a song or two before putting money in the tip jar. They played classic gospel songs like *When the Saints Go Marching In,* and *I'll Fly Away.* Daniel was happy I knew the lyrics to them, and when he commented on it, I told him just because I hadn't been raised going to church didn't mean I wasn't a student of all types of music.

This got us into conversation about God. He said he didn't understand how people could face the certain hardships of this life without relying on God. I could feel that during the conversation he was on the very verge of sharing with me about his accident, but he didn't do it.

We had an extremely eventful day, and it was past dinnertime when we decided to go back to the room. I called for room service before heading into my bedroom to take a shower. Afterward, I changed into tights and a comfortable sweatshirt and left my long, blonde hair hanging in damp waves over my shoulders.

By the time I came back into the main room, our food had arrived. Daniel was in the kitchen, looking at everything we had ordered. He had taken a shower as well and was now wearing a pair of dark sweatpants with a fitted, athletic T-shirt. I approached him, smiling and thinking he looked like a professional soccer player.

"Hey, Courtney's back," he said, grinning at me as I came to stand next to him.

"Did you really think you were on a date with somebody else all day?"

He pulled back and glanced at me like he wasn't quite sure what to think about me calling our day a date.

"Do you think I do stuff like that with Trevor?" I asked, cutting to the chase.

"I hope not."

"Okay then, don't look at me so funny when I call it a date."

Daniel pulled back and took a deep breath, running a hand through his dark hair.

"What?" I asked.

"Where's Denise?" he asked, glancing at the door as if he were afraid she would walk in any second.

I took a mini crab cake off of the plate and popped it into my mouth. "She's still with her boyfriend's cousin," I said as I chewed. "She texted me earlier. They're going out to see some music tonight."

Daniel shifted so that he could lean against the countertop.

"What?" I said.

"I guess it's just… I guess I just feel like it's time for me to go ahead and tell you that I can't make you any promises. I, uh, I really don't date women. I don't date."

I remembered what his sister told me, but I pretended not to since I wasn't supposed to know. Instead, I cocked my head to the side and gave him a surprised and curious expression. "What do you mean?"

"I mean that if I could be tempted to date a person in this universe, Courtney, it would be you. You would be the one. But I just don't date. I can't do it. I don't do it." He hesitated, taking a deep contemplative breath, and I watched as he touched his stomach.

"Tell me what's going on, Daniel," I said coming to stand in front of him.

He wouldn't look at me—he stared to the side.

"Daniel," I said, moving in front of his line of vision to try to get him to make eye contact. He finally did, and I could see the pain in his eyes.

"I'm not able to make any commitments, Courtney. You're beautiful and wonderful, and I want so badly to act on my impulses, but I can't. I have some stuff from way back that I carry around with me. I just can't do it. I like you, but I can't promise you anything. It wouldn't be fair to you, and it wouldn't be fair to... other people."

"What are you talking about? What do you carry around with you?" I asked.

"Stuff. Things from my past."

"I thought you told me you know God, and that He helps you get through stuff."

"I do, and He does. There are just some things that have consequences that never go away... there are just some boundaries I don't cross."

I could see that he was pulling away from me, and I felt so mad that tears sprang to my eyes. I knew he could see my eyes beginning to water, and I didn't care. I just sat there and stared at him as my vision became blurry.

"Why do you have to make me go and get feelings for you, then?"

"I didn't try to make you get feelings for me. I tried my best to make you *not* get feelings for me."

"If that's what you're trying to do, then you are terrible at it. You stink at it, Daniel. I have all sorts of feelings."

Chapter 9

Things got slightly tense after our conversation in the kitchen. I didn't want it that way, so I told him we could take a step back and just go back to enjoying our time together with no more mention of it being a date. Daniel agreed to that, and was only slightly quieter than before.

I had rooftop access with my suite, and the space up there felt like a Spanish courtyard with terra-cotta tiles and a beautiful fountain. We took our food out there and enjoyed the evening view of New Orleans.

We talked about different things we had encountered throughout the day, from musicians, to street performers, to just watching the action on the street from a bench.

We had stopped for a milkshake earlier in the day at a small diner, and we met a waiter by the name of Peanut. He had an electric personality and had been working at the diner for a really long time, so he knew most everyone who came in. Even if he didn't know them, he acted like he did. I was relatively sure Peanut had never met a stranger. At one point, he had the whole place singing *If You're Happy and You Know It*, and Daniel and I laughed at the memory of the whole restaurant clapping along.

Both of us agreed that our day in New Orleans had been one of the most memorable experiences of our lives.

"The only problem is that I didn't get to dance," I said.

Daniel glanced at me. "What do you mean?"

"That's the only thing our day was missing," I said.

"Dancing?" he asked.

I nodded.

"I can't help you on that one," he said.

"Oh, come on. You dance, don't you?"

He shook his head.

"You can't come to New Orleans and not dance.

He let out a little laugh. "Oh, yes I can."

"That's terrible."

"I thought we just talked about what a good day we had."

"I know, but that's before I remembered we were missing something."

He shook his head, giving me a little smile. "I don't think we're missing anything."

"Well, I want to dance," I said.

He shrugged. "I'll go with you if you want to go somewhere, but I think you should wear that curly hair again. That worked well today. And just so you know, I'm not dancing."

"I don't want to dance with anyone else," I said.

He chuckled again. "Well, I'm sorry, but I don't dance. That's one thing I don't do. I'm pretty sure you have about fifty professional dancers staying in this hotel who would all be willing to come out with us if you need a partner."

"I don't want to go anywhere," I said. "I want to stay here."

I smiled at him before I popped up, leaving him sitting on the couch on the rooftop terrace. I went into the room and turned on the stereo system. I had stayed there before, so I knew right where everything was and how to turn it on. I selected a playlist called 'Slow Jazz,' and made sure that it was being channeled through the rooftop speakers.

By the time I made it back on to the terrace, Daniel could hear the music, and he was smiling at me and shaking his head. "How did you do that?" he asked.

I shrugged and smiled as I made my way toward him. I stopped in front of him holding out my hand as if asking him to dance, and he reluctantly gave me his hand as he stood up.

"When you said you wanted to go dancing, I imagined hip-hop moves like you do in your show," he said.

I laughed. "You thought that I wanted to go out and get busy at a club or something?"

"Yes," he said, situating in front of me and regarding me with a teasing grin.

"Did you think I was asking you to take me out clubbing when I'm already in my comfy clothes?" I glanced down at my sweatshirt and tights, and Daniel scanned me from head to toe.

"You could wear a canvas sack and still look amazing," he said.

I grinned and snuggled up close to him in a 'dancing position' where I put my right arm around his waist and grabbed his hand with my left. I didn't even give him the chance to deny me; I just began swaying slowly to the music while I rested my head on his chest. I breathed in the smell of him, feeling utterly relieved to finally be in his arms. I should've thought of this dancing thing way sooner.

I didn't look at him. I was afraid if I did he would say something or stop dancing, so I just held onto him and moved slowly to the music. There was electricity flowing from my fingertips and face and wherever else our bodies made contact. I felt safe, secure, relieved, and altogether breathless.

We stood there, holding each other and gently swaying while the music played. Two songs had passed before I finally spoke. "I don't care if you can't promise me anything," I said.

Daniel didn't reply right away, but I knew he heard me, so I continued.

"I don't need you to make any promises, and I don't need us to give a name to what's going on between us. I just wanted to dance with you. I just wanted to be close to you."

Saying those words to him made me feel vulnerable and tingly inside, and I held onto him a little tighter as I spoke. His chest expanded as he took a slow deep breath, and I rested my face against him, wishing I could stay there forever.

"I have a brother," he said. He stopped swaying to the music, and I pulled back just far enough to look at him, but I didn't let him go.

"I know," I said with a smile. "You have two of them. Owen and Wesley."

Music played in the background, and we could hear some sounds of the city, but I just stood there, staring into his dark eyes. I already knew what he was trying to tell me, and I was nervous because of it.

"It's Owen I'm talking about—my brother Owen."

"What about him?"

I hated pretending that I didn't know, but I also didn't want to get Ivy in trouble for telling me.

"He was in an accident when he was ten years old, and he lost his foot. He lost his right foot and the bottom part of his right leg. He still has his knee and a couple of inches below the knee, but every morning when he wakes up, he has to put it on this prosthetic leg with a fake foot. It's a complicated contraption with a vacuum pump and layers of silicone that fit onto what's left of his leg."

"I'm sorry," I said. I wanted to ask what happened, but I felt bad doing that since I already knew. "I hate to hear that."

"He's also got a big scar down the side of his face." Daniel turned to the side and slowly traced a line with his finger from his eyebrow, all the way down his cheek to the bottom of his jaw.

I could see the pain in Daniel's eyes when he traced the line of that scar, and my heart ached for him. There was so much I wanted to say, but I opted to just stand there and give Daniel time to work out whatever he wanted to tell me.

He sighed. "I guess I've always felt like Owen will be limited in life because of his leg." He paused and gave me a sad smile before continuing. "He's young, and he's got a lot going for him, so I'm sure he'll be able to find someone who loves him for who he is, but it is what it is. Owen is the Bishop brother who has a scar down his face and only one leg."

"Is Owen the reason why you don't date?" I asked.

Daniel was lost in thought as he gave me a slight nod. He still hadn't told me that he was the one responsible for the accident. He vaguely hinted at it, but he hadn't come out and said it. I could honestly tell it was because he thought that piece of information would make me feel differently about him. I wanted to say something to reassure him, but I couldn't. I had to just let him tell me what he wanted to share when he wanted to share it.

I placed my hands on the sides of his face, gently urging him to look straight at me. "Daniel," I said softly. "I'm not going to pretend to know everything about you. I'm not going to pretend to know all of your feelings or past, or what goes into all of the choices you make." I let my hands drop from his face, wrapping them around his waist once again. I took a deep breath as I stared at his handsome, stoic face. "Just know that I honestly don't care what you can promise me," I continued. "I don't need you to tell me that you're going to take me back home to meet your family. Owen doesn't even have to know I exist. I don't need you to promise me anything. I'm not asking anything of you beyond this moment right here. I just want to kiss you, that's all."

He scanned my face, letting his eyes roam over every part of it, taking special interest in my mouth.

"You're giving me no other choice but to do it," he said.

I could tell he wanted to; I could see the primal desire in his eyes.

"Good," I whispered. I was absolutely buzzing with anticipation. I looked from his eyes to his mouth and back to his eyes again, wishing so badly that he would just go ahead and do it.

"You're the most beautiful creature I've ever seen in my life, Courtney. I think you might be the prettiest thing God ever created."

He genuinely meant it, and the sincerity of his words touched my heart. I had been around a lot of famous people during my career. I had seen a lot of handsome faces, and even kissed a few leading men, but Daniel was different. He was a strikingly handsome man, and he wasn't afraid to take control of situations in other aspects of life, but matters of the heart were different. He was innocent and reluctant—I could see the underlying fear in his eyes, waging war with his desire.

"You're not going to kiss me, are you?" I asked. I was desperate for it to happen, and it broke my heart to say that, but I feared it was the truth.

"I can't," he said. "I don't know how."

My heart dropped at his words. "Have you never kissed a woman, Daniel?"

He gave me an almost imperceptible shake of the head as he stared at me.

"No?" I asked.

He shook his head again.

"Never, in your whole life?"

Another slight shake.

"Not even a peck?"

He shook his head again as he stared at me.

"Seriously?"

He nodded.

And there was nothing I could do to stop tears from rising to my eyes. *How in the world could a man who looked like this go his whole life without kissing a woman? How was that even possible?*

"Why are you crying?" he asked, reaching up to wipe my cheek with his thumb.

I gave him a little shrug because, the truth was, I didn't know exactly why I was crying. I was just so overwhelmed with emotion for Daniel Bishop that tears rose to my eyes.

"Maybe it's because I get to be the first," I said.

He gave me a little grin. "So, they're happy tears?"

I nodded.

"Thank goodness," he said. "I thought maybe you were dreading it now."

"Dreading what? Kissing you?" I asked incredulously.

He gave me a little nod. "You know… because I don't have experience. I might not be very good at it."

"That's the furthest thing from my mind," I said. "If anything, I'm worried *I'll* disappoint you."

He smiled sweetly at me. "That could never happen."

Chapter 10

I couldn't stop myself from shaking as Daniel and I stood on the terrace discussing our eminent kiss. I had mixed emotions. I wanted to kiss him, but he was so precious and pure and wonderful that I hardly knew where to begin.

Both of us were struggling to catch our breath, and all we were doing was standing there, looking at each other.

"Are you cold?" he asked, pulling me a little closer. I shook my head as I stared up at him.

"You're shaking."

"I can't help it," I said.

Daniel left one hand around my waist, and with the other, he reached up, touching the hair near my temple. "You're perfect," he whispered.

I smiled. "No, I'm not. Far from it."

He moved his hand, cupping the side of my face and letting his thumb touch my lip. I turned to the side so that I could kiss his thumb, placing an open-mouthed kiss right on the tip of it. I watched him watch me do it. He stared right at the place where his thumb met my lips.

"Oh my gosh, Courtney," he said. He held the side of my face and stared longingly at me as if I was something truly precious—almost as if I was breakable. The truth was, I felt breakable.

"Daniel," I whispered. "I'm going to kiss your lips, okay?"

He regarded me seriously as he gave me a slight nod. "Okay," he said.

I slowly brought my hands to his face again, and as I stretched upward to kiss him, he leaned down to let his lips fall on mine with complete and utter tenderness. My knees went weak and I melted in his arms the instant we made contact. His lips were as soft and pure as I imagined they would be. I let out a whimper and then kissed him again softly, two, three, four times. His lips were perfect and untouched, and I was out-of-my-head with desire for him.

I broke the kiss, and I started to say something about how he had no business worrying about his inexperience, but he denied me by shaking his head to tell me he wasn't finished. This caused an instant crashing wave of anticipation to hit me, and without hesitation, I stretched up to kiss him again. This time, I took his bottom lip into my mouth. The warmth of his open mouth was too much for me. I let out another whimpering sound just before I opened my mouth to him.

And Daniel Bishop kissed me deeply.

He kept one hand around my waist and wrapped the other one around the back of my head pulling me close and kissing me like we had done it a thousand times. It was a good thing he was holding onto me because I could hardly stand on my own. In those glorious seconds, Daniel held me tightly and kissed me passionately like I was his and he was mine and nothing would ever come between us.

I didn't know how much time had passed when Daniel finally broke the kiss and pulled back. Both of us were struggling to regulate our breathing more than ever, and we grinned at each other.

"There's no way you've never done that before," I said.

He smiled. "You must be a good teacher."

I let my fingertips roam along the side of his head through his hair and then along the side of is face. "Do you promise that was the first time you ever did that?" I asked. I still felt like it couldn't possibly be true.

He let out a little laugh. "Yes," he said. "I promise. Gabby Anderson kissed me at summer camp one time, but I was sleeping, and when I woke up I—"

Daniel stopped talking when I closed my eyes and shook my head, telling him I didn't want to hear anymore about Gabby Anderson. "Please don't make me hate some poor girl I don't even know. Just tell me that was the first time."

"It was the first time," Daniel said seriously.

Both of us held onto each other.

"You're still shaking," he said, rubbing my arms and using friction to warm me up. "Are you sure you're not cold?"

"I promise I'm not cold," I said. "But we can go inside if you want."

Daniel and I went inside and made ourselves comfortable on the couch in the living room. We turned on the television, but neither of us paid attention to it. Instead, we talked. He told me more about his family, his parents, siblings, cousins, and grandparents. He alluded to Owen's accident again, but again, he didn't tell me that he had been the one responsible for it.

He told me more about his job at Alpha, and we laughed at some of the misadventures he had with the guys who were just starting to train. His uncle Gray, who was also his boss and mentor, had a brother named Kevin Kennedy who was a famous comedian. Kevin had a successful sitcom in the early nineties, and Daniel's cousin, Shelby, had starred on it when she was younger. I remembered meeting her years ago at an awards show, and we marveled at what a small world it was.

Daniel was curious about my time on the road, and I told him stories of experiences I had in other countries and in various cities in the U.S. We laughed and talked for hours that night, and I had it in my mind that I was going to kiss him again, but Denise came in from her night out, foiling my plans. She sat up with us for a little while, telling us about her night on the town, before we all decided that it was time to get some rest.

I replayed and overanalyzed everything Daniel and I had said to each other when I was trying to fall asleep. It had been such a long day that was so full of action and conversation that it was difficult for me to remember everything—I kept thinking of details I had forgotten.

Every time I closed my eyes, I could picture our kiss on the rooftop. It was still so real to me that it gave me butterflies, causing me to smile and shift around in my bed even though I was completely alone in my room.

I thought about the way I told Daniel that he didn't have to promise me anything, and I already regretted it. I *wanted* promises from him, and I was mad at myself for assuring him I didn't need them. It truly made me sad that Daniel didn't think he deserved to find love, and I convinced myself that I would be the one to eventually change his mind.

***

We had gone to bed late, so I didn't wake up until almost 10 the following morning. Normally, I might stay in bed for a half-hour just being lazy and thinking about what I had to do that day, but I was so excited to see Daniel that I hopped up after only a couple of minutes.

I stepped into my slippers and walked into the living room with a smile on my face. My heart sank when I realized that Daniel and Denise weren't alone. They were sitting at the table with Trevor.

100

I blinked, thinking I might be seeing things. "Heyyyy," I said, trying my best not to act disappointed.

Trevor stood up and came toward me the instant he noticed me. His arms were outstretched, and he was wearing a huge grin. "I'm alive!" he said.

"Yayyy!" I said, doing my best to act genuinely excited.

We walked toward each other, and I gave him a relieved hug. "What happened?" I asked. "How'd you get here so quick?"

"They gave me steroids and antibiotics, and now I feel like a new man. They released me last night, and I got on a flight this morning. I just pulled up a few minutes ago."

Daniel and Denise were still sitting at the table, and Trevor and I walked over there to join them as we talked. I glanced at Daniel, half expecting him to do something crazy like freak out and tell Trevor he was fired, but he just sat there like everything was normal. I made a little face at him that I hoped neither Denise nor Trevor noticed.

I approached the table, and Daniel reached out to pull out a chair for me. It was the one next to him, which made me feel slightly less heartbroken.

"Thank you," I said.

"I'll get your coffee," Denise said, standing as soon as I took a seat.

"You don't have to. I'll get up and get it in a minute."

"It's fine, I don't mind," Denise said.

She busied herself in the kitchen, and Trevor took a seat across from me at the table. I looked at him with a sigh and a smile, doing my best to seem excited. "I'm so happy you feel better," I said. That was the truth, so I knew it came across as sincere.

"I can't believe you got the boss man over here filling in for me," Trevor said, nudging his chin at Daniel. "I thought he was allergic to leaving Memphis."

Daniel smiled and shrugged. "I took some Claritin," he said, causing Trevor to laugh.

"Seriously though, thanks," Trevor said, leaning over the table to give Daniel a sincere hi-five-type maneuver.

"No worries," Daniel said, returning the gesture. "I enjoyed it."

I felt sick to my stomach. I was glad to see Trevor and was happy he was feeling better, but I knew it meant Daniel would be leaving, and the thought of it made me physically sick.

"Denise was telling me that all you have is a phone interview today," Trevor said, regarding me.

I nodded. "Yep. Then sound check at four."

"Daniel told me you drug him all over the city yesterday," Trevor said, kicking back and putting his hands behind his head in a totally relaxed pose. "I guess that means you're gonna want to take it easy today."

"Yep," I said.

I glanced at Daniel who shook his head almost imperceptibly at me. Trevor must have noticed that I was a little annoyed because he spoke up when he saw the way I looked at Daniel.

"He didn't say you *drug him around*," Trevor explained. "I was just kidding about that. I asked him what you guys did, and he told me some of the highlights."

"I bet he didn't tell you *everything*," I said, feeling hurt, stubborn, and brave.

I stared at Daniel who regarded me with an unreadable expression.

"What'd you leave out?" Trevor asked curiously.

"I don't know," Daniel said innocently. "I thought I covered just about everything.

"Did you tell him we sang *If You're Happy and You Know It* at the diner with Peanut?"

Trevor's eyebrows rose as he gave me a perplexed expression like he had no idea what that sentence meant.

"I might have left that out," Daniel said. "I forgot about that part."

I squinted at Daniel like I was mad at him for saying he forgot any of it, and he smiled at me and give me a little confident shake of the head.

"Did you tell him you taught me Jiu-Jitsu?" I asked challengingly.

Right when I asked the question, Denise set a mug of coffee in front of me, so I turned to her and said, "Thank you. Could you possibly get me a bottled water and that peppermint oil?"

Denise gave me a quick nod and took off toward her room.

"He taught you *Jiu-Jitsu*?" Trevor asked. He sounded and looked astonished, and Daniel grinned at him and shook his head.

"I showed her a cross-choke," he explained.

"Oh, that's good," Trevor said, nodding with an approving smile.

"I was really good at it," I said. "I choked him on the first try."

I held my coffee mug close to my chest and breathed in the smell of it, but I didn't take a sip—I was too nauseated for that.

Trevor laughed. "You better not train her too much or she won't need us anymore."

Denise brought me the bottled water and peppermint oil, and I set my coffee down so I could add a drop to it just like Daniel taught me.

"What's that?" Trevor asked.

"Daniel bought it for her," Denise said, sitting down with us. "He said it would help her ulcer." She glanced at me with a look of concern. "I have your prescription in my room if you need it."

"You're knocking it out of the park," Trevor said, teasing Daniel. "Training Jiu-Jitsu... bringing her medicine... I better be careful not to get sick again."

He was only kidding, of course, so we all laughed.

"I still don't understand what you're saying about being *happy at a diner*, though."

"Peanut," I said. I took a sip of my peppermint water, praying that it worked on heartache as well. "We ate at a diner yesterday, and we had a waiter who made us sing. We sang, *If You're Happy and You Know It*, and the whole place was clapping and stomping."

Trevor shook his head, looking at Daniel. "You're brave, letting her sing in public. Stuff like that sets people going crazy and calling their friends."

"It wasn't like that," I said. "No one knew who I was. I just sat on the stool and sang along with everybody else."

Trevor smiled and continued to shake his head at us like we were brave, crazy, or both. "Sounds like y'all had fun," he said. He reached across the table to shake Daniel's hand again. "Thanks again, brother. I really appreciate you filling in for me."

"It really wasn't a problem," Daniel said.

He glanced at me. He still wore an unreadable expression. I knew he wasn't happy about leaving me, but I was frustrated that he wasn't doing anything about it. I wanted him to turn over the table in anger and refuse to go anywhere.

I took another sip of the peppermint water, reminding myself that was ridiculous and I should be happy to see Trevor.

Chapter 11
Daniel

Assuming that Daniel would want to get home as soon as possible, Lydia, the secretary at Alpha, booked him a flight out of New Orleans that very same afternoon.

Daniel should have been relieved about this, but he absolutely dreaded leaving Courtney's side. He felt protective of her, and not just in a professional way. He wanted to shield her from any and every hardship life threw her way. She had come into his life and completely rocked his world.

She sat next to him at the breakfast table, doing her best to pretend she was excited to see Trevor. He could see the underlying sadness in her expression, and he wanted so badly to reach out and take her into his arms.

He imagined moments from their encounters, thinking about how funny and sweet she was and remembering the feel of her soft lips on his. He was completely swept away by Courtney Cole. She caused him to have feelings he had never felt before.

He caught himself thinking that he didn't care what Owen felt or if he liked it or not, and he had to repent of those feelings, knowing he would regret them once he got home and was face-to-face with his brother. It killed him, but he knew it was best for everybody if he just went back Memphis and resumed his life as it was before he met Courtney.

Courtney stayed in the main area with the rest of them for a little while before excusing herself to take a shower. Daniel assumed she would come back out before he left for the airport, but she stayed in her room for the next two hours. He knew there was a driver on his way to pick him up, but he didn't feel like he could leave without telling her goodbye.

Trevor and Denise were both still sitting in the living room, and Daniel didn't really care what they thought about it when he said, "I've got to go downstairs in a few minutes, so I'm going to knock on Courtney's door to tell her goodbye."

"I'll see what she's doing," Denise said, standing up to take charge of the situation. She crossed to Courtney's door and gave it a few light knocks.

"Yeah?"

Daniel was standing close enough that he could hear her muffled voice through the door, and his heart ached to be next to her.

"Daniel is on his way to the airport," Denise said speaking towards the edge of the closed door. "He wanted to say goodbye." Denise turned and gave Daniel a little smirk and shrug as if she had no idea how Courtney would respond to this proposition.

"I thought he already left," he heard Courtney say from the other side of the door.

Denise stared at Daniel. "He's about to. He's standing right here."

There was a long silence, after which Courtney said, "You can let him come in."

Denise moved to the side, and Daniel stepped in front of her, opening the door slowly and cautiously. He expected Courtney to be up and around, and he was surprised to find her in bed with the covers pulled up to her chin. She was on her side staring toward the window, and he walked over there to sit beside her. He perched on the edge of the bed near her legs, feeling heartbroken that she wouldn't look at him.

"Are you feeling okay?" he asked.

"Not really," she said.

He reached out and rubbed the back of her legs in a comforting manner. She was under the covers, so he could barely feel her, but he had to touch her one last time. "Denise said she has a prescription for your stomach," he said.

"I'm fine. I'll ask her for it if I need it."

"I didn't want to leave without saying goodbye," he said.

"Okay," she said, still staring blankly at the wall.

He rubbed her legs again. He could see that she didn't want to talk to him, but he couldn't just leave things this way. He had to say something sincere.

"Courtney, I had a really good time with you."

"Thanks," she said without taking her head off the pillow or looking at him.

Several seconds passed where Daniel tried to convince himself that he should just stand up and walk out, but he couldn't do it.

"I didn't know Trevor was going to be here this morning," he said. "I was just as surprised as you were when he walked in."

"I'm glad he feels better," she said. "It's good to have him back."

"Then why are you upset?"

"I'm not upset," she said. "These are my normal stomach issues. It happens every time I'm on tour, especially toward the end like this. I just have to lay here and rest until it's time to go to the venue."

"Would you let me pray for you?" he asked.

"If you want," she said, still not looking at him.

Daniel scooted up, positioning himself where he was sitting next to her waist. He turned to put his hand on her back, realizing that she had closed her eyes. He kept his eyes open, watching her as he began to pray.

"Father, You created Courtney. You formed her with Your own hands. You love her, and You know exactly what's going on in her body." Daniel paused when he saw tears begin to stream out of the corners of her closed eyes. "Please, Lord, help her. Touch her body. Give her strength to finish this road trip. You are the Great Physician. You are the Almighty God. Touch her and help her complete the job she has started. Give her wellness, and help her to know how very much she is loved. It's in Jesus's name we pray, Amen."

Courtney kept her eyes closed, but Daniel watched as tears streamed off of her face and fell onto the pillow. He reached up and put a loving hand on the back of her head.

"Thank you," she whispered.

"I'm sorry you don't feel well."

"It's fine," she said. "I just have two more shows."

"My driver is on his way," Daniel said.

"I know."

"I wish you would look at me," he said, staring at her precious face as he stroked her hair.

She kept her eyes closed.

"Courtney," he whispered, feeling desperate to see her beautiful blue eyes again.

"What?"

"Won't you look at me?"

She didn't.

She just stayed there with her eyes closed.

He stared at her, wishing there was something more he could do. "I was driving that motorcycle," he said, speaking slowly and softly. "I was the one who wrecked it. I took my dad's motorcycle without permission, and I talked Owen into coming with me. Owen's life is changed forever, and it's nobody's fault but mine." Daniel continued to gently rub Courtney's head. She was so precious to him, and she didn't even know it.

"I knew about your accident," she said in a small voice. "Your little sister told me."

Daniel wasn't quite sure what to think about that. Part of him was angry that she knew all along and hadn't said anything, and the other part of him was relieved that she knew about it and still felt compelled to get to know him.

"So, you understand why I can't live my life like normal," he said. "It wouldn't be fair to Owen."

Courtney opened her eyes, looking at him and flooding him with relief. "Do you think it's fair to Owen for you to punish yourself for the rest of your life? Do you think Owen likes to see his brother punish himself on his account?"

Daniel hadn't thought of it that way. "Owen doesn't see it that way," he said. "He has no idea."

"You don't think so?" she asked.

"No, I don't," Daniel said. "It's not like I made a big statement telling him what I'm doing or why. He thinks I'm just living my life."

"All right then, I guess you know what you're doing," she said with a sad smile.

Daniel rubbed her head again, touching the side of her beautiful face as she closed her tear-filled eyes. She was like an exquisite porcelain doll, and he knew he would never get past the guilt if he let himself enjoy such a beautiful prize in life. It made him sick to leave her, but he knew he had to do it.

"Courtney, I want you to know that I will never forget what happened last night. It was a moment of pure magic in my life, and I will lock that memory in my heart and hang onto it forever."

Tears streamed out of her eyes again, but she remained still and said nothing.

"Please know how special you are." He stared at her, wishing she would look at him.

"You better go," she said. "I have that phone interview in just a little while, and I have to get up and get my brain straight for that."

He let out a sigh. "Okay," he said. He stood up to leave her but he couldn't bear to do it. He leaned down and placed a lingering kiss on the side of her forehead.

Earlier, when she had been crying, her face hadn't moved at all, there were just wet tears running out of her eyes with no change of facial expression. But this time, when Daniel leaned down to kiss her, her face crumpled with tears like it caused her pain.

"I'm sorry," he whispered.

She shook her head. "Just go."

Daniel stood up, turned around, and left the room without another word. He spoke with Denise and Trevor on his way out, and then he spoke with the driver on the way to the airport, but it was like he was in a dream—a nightmare. He had experienced the pain of guilt and heartache for most of his life, but he had never loved a woman the way he loved Courtney, and the pain of finding her and then losing her was almost unbearable.

***

In the days that followed, Daniel was in a terrible mood. Everyone at Alpha assumed he was cross for having to fill in for Trevor, and he just let them believe that. He threw himself into training because the only relief he could find was when he worked his body to the point of physical exhaustion.

He was so sick over it that he ignored phone calls from his family until his mother finally got worried enough to knock on his door and check on him. Ivy came with her, and she was really curious about his time with Courtney, so she asked him what must have been a hundred questions about their time together.

Daniel was obviously not in the mood for such questions, and the two women left his house assuming that he developed feelings for the pop singer. He didn't really care what they thought; he just wanted to get through enough days until the memory of Courtney faded and he could get back to his life.

Daniel was in a grocery store doing some much-needed shopping when he experienced something utterly amazing. He was in the milk aisle, trying to decide whether he should get two-percent or whole when he heard an audible voice say, "Daniel, go to Dallas."

His head whipped around, and he stared at the lady next to him who was holding a container of yogurt. It was a man's voice that he had heard, and she was clearly a lady, but she was the only other person nearby.

"Excuse me?" he asked.

She smiled curiously at him.

"What did you say?" he asked.

She put a hand to her chest. "Me? I didn't say anything."

The words we're clearly audible and someone had said them plain as day, but this lady regarded Daniel with a look of surprise and confusion.

"Did you say something about Dallas?" he asked.

She shook her head. "No. I didn't say anything," she said innocently.

"Did you hear someone say 'go to Dallas'?" He asked.

"Nooo," she said with a wide-eyed expression. "I definitely didn't hear that."

Daniel looked over his shoulder in the other direction, making sure that they were alone on the aisle. He was tired from a long day at work, but he had no doubt about what he heard. The words were clear, unmistakable, and spoken out loud.

"Did a man's voice come over the intercom?" he asked.

The lady had looked away, but she looked at him again. "Just now, you mean? While we were standing here?"

He nodded.

"Not that I heard." She pointed upward. "I think it's just been playing music."

"And you didn't hear anyone say anything?"

She shook her head, looking perplexed and maybe even starting to look a little wary.

Daniel smiled, doing his best to appear sane and act as if he wasn't hearing things.

"Thanks," he said. "Must have been my phone."

Daniel paid for his groceries while doing his best to appear unrattled, but he knew what he heard, and he couldn't get it out of his mind. He tried to remember if anyone he knew had ever heard from God in a clear voice. His family had experienced different things like dreams or feelings, but he couldn't think of a single example of someone who had heard God speak audibly.

For a minute, Daniel tried to convince himself that he was just hearing what he wanted to hear. He knew Courtney was in Dallas and he told himself his mind was playing tricks on him.

But he knew that wasn't the truth. He knew in his heart what he had heard. He knew it was a real voice. He left the store, knowing that he was about to pack his bags and leave for Dallas.

Chapter 12
Courtney
Dallas, TX

I collapsed into Trevor's arms the instant I sang the final note and stepped backstage. It was my last show on the tour, and I had given the performance literally everything I had in me.

I waved and smiled at the crowd on my way off the stage, and the next thing I knew, I was falling. I was vaguely aware of people hustling around and talking about whether or not I needed to go to a hospital or if I could just get by with having a doctor come to my hotel room. I didn't care for hospitals, so I made a real effort to respond to the questions in such a way that let them know I was okay and didn't need to go to one.

We got into the back of a car, and I listened to Denise's phone conversation in which she made arrangements for a doctor to meet us at the hotel. I heard her talking to my publicist, Gina, on the phone before telling Trevor that it was better if we could take care of this at the hotel rather than at a hospital.

I had experienced all of these physical symptoms before, so I told myself I'd be okay, but it never got easy to feel weak, dizzy, and nauseous. I was completely out of it and just had to trust that the doctor would be able to make me feel better.

I remember bits and pieces of the car ride and the trip into the hotel and up the elevator. I walked on my own because I knew if I would have asked Trevor to carry me like I wanted him to, they would have brought me to the hospital.

We had a doctor come to my room a few times in the past, so Denise knew exactly what to tell them. She mentioned more than once that I was dehydrated and needed fluids.

Thankfully, he was already waiting in the room when we got there. He was dressed in plain clothes and he introduced himself as Dr. Thomas. I answered his questions, and before I knew it, I was stretched out on my bed with an IV attached to my arm.

Dr. Thomas had a kind, quiet bedside manner, and I trusted him to do what he could to help me feel better. Denise worked at taking my shoes off, taking my hair down, and making me more comfortable.

The next few hours passed in a dreamy haze.

The last thing I remembered before dozing off was Dr. Thomas telling me he would be in the next room if I needed anything.

It was one o'clock in the morning when I glanced at the clock and realized that I might just live to see another day. I glanced at the IV bag, which was almost empty. I watched it dripping slowly, feeling thankful for whatever it was putting into my body.

I realized I could hear voices in the other room.

It sounded like they were agitated.

I looked around my room, noticing that I was alone. I listened closely, trying to hear what the voices were saying—wondering what anyone could possibly be arguing about.

"He cares about her," a man's voice said. (I thought it was Trevor, but I couldn't be sure.) "He's not gonna bother her. He just wants to stay in here with us."

"It's really nice that he cares about her," I heard Denise say. "But it's one o'clock in the morning. Tell him he can get a room and come by in the morning. She's in no shape for visitors right now."

"He's standing at the door," Trevor said. "What am I supposed to tell him?"

"Tell him to get a room," Denise said. "We've got our hands full in here."

I realized it was Trevor and Denise arguing, and I tried my hardest to figure out what they were concerned about. I tilted my head toward the door as I listened closely. I wondered if they might be talking about the doctor.

"I like him and everything, Trevor, but tonight's not the night for Court to have visitors. We're about to go to bed, anyway. He can come back in the morning if he wants to see her."

"Denise, all he wants to do is sit out here in a chair. He's not hurting anything. He cares about her. He came all the way from Memphis to see her."

My heart started pounding the instant I heard the word *Memphis*.

"Who?" I yelled.

My mouth was incredibly dry and my voice barely came out, so I yelled again.

"Who's here?"

Seconds later, I saw my door crack open. Denise came in with an apologetic look on her face—I could see her clearly because the light in my bathroom was on.

"Did we wake you up?" she asked regretfully. "I'm so sorry if we did."

"Who's here?"

"Trevor's been talking to the other guy from Alpha, Daniel. He said he came over here to—"

"Where is he?" I asked cutting her off. "Where's Daniel? Is he here?"

"He's not in the room or anything. It's just Trevor and me. Dr. Thomas went downstairs to get some coffee. How are you feeling?"

"I want Daniel," I said.

I knew I should probably say something more eloquent, but I was still exhausted, and the simple truth was the only thing I could think to say.

Denise looked at me like she was a little confused.

"Please get Daniel," I said. "I want him in here with me right now."

Denise still looked a bit skeptical as she turned around and headed for the door. I heard her say something to Trevor and then I heard some other noises including footsteps and the sound of a door opening.

And within seconds, I saw Daniel step into the room. Instantly, my eyes flooded with relieved tears. I felt so overwhelmed with joy that I held out my arms, inviting Daniel to hug me from his position all the way on the other side of the room.

I watched as Daniel crossed the room with a determined look on his face. He didn't stop until he took me into his arms. He sat on the edge of my bed and leaned over me, wrapping himself around me like a glorious, protective shield.

He held me tightly for several long seconds before he pulled back just far enough to put a kiss on the side of my face. He did it two or three more times, kissing my cheek and hairline with as much relief and happiness as I was feeling.

"I'm sorry," he whispered in my ear. "I'm sorry I wasn't here with you."

My eyes were blurry with tears, but I could see that Denise and Trevor were both standing in the doorway, watching us with great curiosity. I didn't have the strength to explain what was going on or even care what they were thinking. I focused on Daniel, taking his handsome face in my hands and telling myself I was not dreaming and that he was actually sitting there.

"You came," I whispered. "You're here."

He smiled at me and reached up to smooth my hair. I saw him glance at my arm, and then follow the IV line up to the bag of fluid. "I'm so sorry you got sick," he said.

"It's okay," I said. "I feel better now."

Daniel let go of me just long enough to kick off his shoes and climb around me and onto the bed. He stacked a couple of pillows next to me and sat down with his legs stretched out as if he didn't plan on going anywhere. I watched him complete the whole maneuver, and by the time he was finished, I turned to find Denise standing at my bedside. I gave her a sleepy smile.

"You okay?" she asked, referring to the fact that Daniel had just made himself at home next to me.

I smiled and nodded. "I want him here," I said.

"The doctor just went downstairs for a second. He'll come check on you when he gets back," she said.

I nodded. "That's fine. I'm fine. Daniel will come get you if I need anything."

Denise was still slightly confused, and she smiled reluctantly at me before turning around to head out of the room.

I turned onto my side, snuggling up next to Daniel. He put his arm around me, creating a spot for me to lay my head on his chest. The soft, familiar smell of sandalwood comforted me greatly.

"I prayed," I said.

"You did?" he asked.

I nodded without even looking at him. "I had to. I didn't know what else to do. I was sicker than I'd ever been before a show. It seemed impossible for me to get through it. I'm so glad it's over." I touched my stomach. I was still a little nauseous, but nothing like I had been earlier.

Daniel rubbed my shoulder comfortingly. "Trevor told me none of the crew even knew anything was bothering you. He said you were a soldier out there."

I smiled against his chest. "I'm so happy you're here."

"You won't believe what prompted me to come," he said.

His statement made me so curious that I lifted my head to glance at him. I was tired and sleepy, and it showed, so Daniel put his hand on my head, encouraging me to relax and rest. "I'd been thinking about you since I left, but this afternoon I was standing in a grocery store when I heard a man say my name and tell me to go to Dallas."

I picked up my head again to stare at him curiously. "Who was it?" I asked, wanting to thank this man.

Daniel regarded me seriously as he shrugged. "No one had said it—at least no one in the store. But it was real and clear, and I heard it with my own ears. So I left there, packed a bag, and went straight to the airport. I called Trevor, and he told me where you guys were staying."

"Do you think it was God?" I asked, resting on his chest again.

"It had to be," he said. "The only other thing I could think of was that it was my subconscious, but I've never had anything like that happen before. It was loud, and I heard it with my own ears."

"That's crazy," I said. "That makes me feel like God really loves me if He did that."

"He does love you," Daniel said.

He held me there for a minute while I imagined him in the grocery store having that whole experience. The thought of it made me smile.

I heard noises from the other room and saw through the crack in the door that the doctor had returned from getting coffee. He and Denise were positioned where I could see them, and I watched as they spoke to each other before heading my way.

Dr. Thomas came to my bedside, but Denise hung back by the door, watching us with sweet concern. He smiled at me before going to work checking my vitals and changing the IV fluids.

"How are you feeling?" he whispered.

"Getting better," I answered. I touched my stomach. "I think whatever you gave me made it not feel so cramped up."

"Great," he said, still fiddling with the IV bag. "How about the nausea?"

"Still there, but it's not as bad," I said.

"Good," he said. He stood by my side, taking in the sight of Daniel lying next to me. "It's really important that you get some rest, Courtney. I wasn't sure if you wanted guests in the room."

"Daniel's not a guest," I said. I reached up to put my hand on his cheek, hoping this act of familiarity would show the doctor how much I cared for him. "He's my boyfriend," I added. "I'm more comfortable with him in here."

Dr. Thomas glanced at Denise with a quick but confused expression, and I watched as Denise tilted her head at me. She had the right to be confused, but I didn't really have the energy to explain.

"Tell them you're my man," I said, shifting to look at Daniel.

"It's true," he said. "I'm here because I love her. I want her to rest, too. I promise I won't keep her up."

The doctor glanced at Denise again who gave him an innocent shrug.

"If you're sure you're comfortable..." he said, looking at me.

"I am," I said. I cozied up next to Daniel, trying to demonstrate just how very comfortable I was. "I'll sleep better with him in here."

"All right," he said. He turned to head for the door. "I'll be here all night. I'm right out here if you need anything."

"Thank you," I said.

"I'm gonna go to bed," Denise said from the door. "Trevor's in his room, too. Just holler if you need us."

I gave her a little smile and wave before both of them disappeared into the living room. I let out a long sigh, feeling so grateful that Daniel was there with me. He was the one person in the world capable of making me feel safe and secure, and I needed that so badly right then.

I yawned. "I've never heard of God talking out loud to anyone," I said.

"Me neither," Daniel said, "Except for in the Bible. But He did it today. I heard it with my own ears."

We were quiet for a few seconds before I whispered, "You told that doctor you love me."

"Yep, I did," he agreed.

"You also let me tell them you're my boyfriend."

"Uh-huh."

The noise of agreement came from his chest, and I smiled at the low sound of it next to my ear. I almost made Daniel confirm that all of that was true and he wasn't just saying it so that they would leave us alone, but I decided I could save those questions for another day. For now, I was content to drift off to sleep.

"I'm happy you're here," I whispered.

"Me too," he said, kissing my forehead.

"Night," I said.

"Night."

Chapter 13

Dr. Thomas stayed in my room the following day. After that, he thought I had recovered enough that he left and told us to call if I needed anything.

The whole crew went back to Los Angeles except for Denise and Trevor who stayed with me. We weren't sure how long I'd need to recover in Dallas, so we sent Anthony home with the tour bus, telling him that the three of us would fly back when I felt up to it.

We ended up staying for three days.

Daniel stayed the whole time. He and I grew even closer during those days when I was holed up in my room recovering, and I knew it would be incredibly difficult to say goodbye when the time came.

We acted like we were together when we were alone in the room, but we toned it down when Denise or Trevor were around just because neither of us felt like answering questions about it. They both knew we had feelings for each other, but we laid off of the PDA when anyone was around, and even when we were alone, we took it really slow.

Both of us wanted to make sure I got back on my feet physically, so we took a little step back from trying to be romantic with each other. It was actually a neat experience for me because I got to see that he truly cared about me and wasn't just interested in me because of physical attraction.

He was kind, compassionate, and patient, but at the same time, he was direct and in control. He was a man's man, and yet somehow so tender toward me.

It was like torture when the time came for us to leave Dallas. I wanted Daniel to just fly back to L.A. with me when we left, but he had to get back to his responsibilities in Memphis.

***

Days passed. I had been apart from him for two weeks, and I missed him more than I thought possible. I swiped one of his shirts out of his bag before we left Dallas, and I loved the fact that it still smelled like him. He knew I had it, but he had no idea that I stuck my face into it every night, breathing in what remained of his sandalwood smell.

I honestly didn't know what was next for Daniel and me. We talked on the phone every day, but we hadn't discussed plans for the future. As far as I was concerned, I should just sell my house in California and move to Memphis, but I hadn't said that to him. I was trying to be patient because I knew he needed that.

Daniel hadn't informed his family about us—and especially not Owen. Of course, I wanted him to do it, but I couldn't blame him for being hesitant. The accident and the guilt from it was something he had held onto for so long that I knew it would take time. He had worked really hard to forgive himself, but he loved Owen so much that it was almost impossible for him to move forward with his life.

Frankly, it was better for me to take things slow, anyway. I had been involved in a few relationships over the years, and the press always had a field day trying to dig up dirt on us. I wanted to spare Daniel that until he was ready.

I stared at my reflection in the mirror, thinking I wish he was ready tonight. Tonight, I was hosting the end of the tour celebration for the whole crew (otherwise known as "the tour party"). I wished more than anything that Daniel could be there to go with me.

Nearly the entire crew would be present and most of them would be bringing a date, so the guest list included nearly two hundred people. It was something I did to thank my crew at the end of every tour, and they always looked forward to it.

I bought goodie bags for everyone, which always included nice gifts like massages and gift cards. I also gave trophies for funny achievements like 'best air-guitar', 'hungriest', 'most calls to their mom', and 'best dental hygiene'. Everyone always loved the awards ceremony because the categories I chose were always truly reflective of the person who deserved it, and this made everyone laugh.

Not every musical artist made it a custom to host an after tour party, but I had been doing it for a number of tours in a row now, and it was always something I looked forward to. After spending so many months together preparing the tour and then taking it on the road, we all felt like family, and it only seemed fitting that we got together to celebrate the team's success.

The album we had been promoting was called Freedom, so the tour party for tonight had affectionately been named "The Freedom Party". We were hosting it in a beautiful hotel ballroom. Denise had hired a party planner to take care of the details, but I would be making a speech and emceeing the award ceremony since that was my favorite part.

I decided to wear a gold dress since it fit the theme we had gone with for costumes on the tour. I wanted Nina and Jake to relax and enjoy their evening at the party, so I had hired someone else to come over and help me get dressed for the event. She had just left my house.

Denise and her boyfriend were riding with me, along with Trevor who still worked full-time for me even at times when we weren't on tour. He was downstairs, and I yelled for him to let Denise and Gabe in when I saw them pull into the driveway.

I took one last look in the mirror before heading downstairs to meet them.

"Look at you!" I said when I caught sight of Denise coming in the door. She was a jeans and T-shirt type of girl. I had seen her wear black slacks on occasion when she really needed to get dressed up, but tonight she looked adorable in a little navy dress.

"This is Gabe's doing," she said, bumping playfully into her boyfriend who smiled and raised his eyebrows.

"Good job, Gabe," I said.

"I don't think I've ever seen her legs," Trevor said, staring at the lower half of Denise as if he was totally perplexed. He was only kidding of course, but Gabe reacted by scowling and fake-punching him for looking at her legs.

"We better go," Denise said. "Trevor's plus-one is waiting for us in the limo."

"Thank y'all for picking her up," Trevor said. "Does she look good?"

"Beautiful," Denise said.

"Trevor's plus-one?" I asked, raising my eyebrows at him for not telling me he was taking someone. "You're bringing a date? Who is she? Why did she wait in the limo? Why didn't she come inside?"

"I told her to wait outside," Trevor said.

We all made our way to the door as I continued to stare at Trevor like I was shocked and disappointed that he hadn't told me about his date.

"She didn't want to come in because she was afraid she looked too much like a man," Denise said once we were outside.

"Like a man?" I asked.

About five different thoughts crossed my mind about Trevor's date and what this statement could've possibly meant. Maybe it was because they went so far as to call Trevor's plus-one a "she" in an effort to trick me, but it never once entered my mind that Daniel would be the one waiting outside.

I was absolutely stunned when I stepped out and saw him at the bottom of the staircase, standing by the limo. He was wearing a smile and a dark suit, and he looked like he was ready for the red carpet.

I stared at him for a few long seconds, feeling like I couldn't possibly get to him fast enough. My heart began racing. I wanted to just melt into nothing and then reappear standing right in front of him.

As much as I tried to think that scenario into existence, it didn't happen. Daniel stood there, smiling and casually leaning against the limo as if he was waiting for me to make the first move, but I was so stunned that I just stayed there, staring at him. He saw my stunned expression and his easy grin broadened as he gestured with his hand for me to come to him.

I had to cross a wide patio before I came to a set of curving stone steps, and I don't even remember doing any of it. I did it as gracefully as possible, but I was in such a hurry that I felt like I might trip with every step.

And just like that, I made it to the limo where Daniel Bishop was standing. I stopped when I was a few feet in front of him. I stared at him, wondering how in the world he was possibly standing right in front of me. I had just talked to him an hour before. I was completely out of breath and not just from my descent down the steps but also from the rush of excitement I felt from seeing him.

"How did you get here?" I asked in between short breaths.

"Denise sent the driver to pick me up at my hotel," he said, wearing a gorgeous amused grin.

"You have a *hotel*? You're staying in a hotel? In my town? In Los Angeles? When'd you get here? How'd you do this?"

The more I rambled the more Daniel's smile broadened, and soon it was just too irresistible. I threw myself into his arms, breathing in the smell of his neck and knowing that his T-shirt had done nothing to represent how he really smelled.

I placed a kiss on his neck before I pulled back and turned around to look at Denise, Gabe, and Trevor who were now headed down the stairs to meet us. I held on to Daniel with my arm wrapped around his waist because I couldn't bear to let him go. He wrapped his arm around my shoulders as if he felt the same way.

I knew we hadn't talked about showing our affection in public, but I couldn't help myself, I missed him so much and was so relieved to see him that I squeezed him tightly and rested my head on his shoulder.

"You guys tricked me," I said, narrowing my eyes at the three others as they approached.

"I guess you're happy to see him," Denise said, stating the obvious.

"I've been working for you for three years, and I never once got that kind of greeting," Trevor said.

"Thank God," Daniel said impassively, causing us all to laugh.

Trevor reached out to shake Daniel's hand, and Daniel let go of me long enough to greet his friend. "Good to see you again, boss," Trevor said. "Even though I'm starting to think I'll be looking for a new gig soon, given the frequency of your visits."

The driver had been hanging back, but he stepped forward to open the door for us, and we all climbed into the limo. Daniel and I sat in the rear seat, facing the front of the car while Denise and Gabe sat on our right and Trevor on our left.

I should've probably been content to sit next to Daniel without making contact, but I couldn't resist reaching out to hold his hand. Feeling a little shy, I tentatively reached out and touched the back of his hand with my fingertips. He glanced at me with a sweet grin before turning over his hand to offer it to me. I gently placed my hand in his, feeling all sorts of nervous anticipation as he closed his fingers.

Chapter 14
Daniel

All these years, Daniel Bishop had no problems keeping his distance from women. It wasn't that he didn't find women attractive, because he did. It's just that his boundaries had been in place for so long that he didn't even consider looking at women in that way.

He was a cute boy who grew into a handsome man, and he had his share of willing, would-be girlfriends over the years, but none of them were even a temptation to him.

That all changed when he met Courtney Cole. She had the capability to tear down walls he didn't even know existed. She somehow made her way through the back door of his heart and took up residence there. She did it so swiftly and subtly that he didn't even know it had happened until it was too late.

He loved her and that's all there was to it.

It wasn't just because she was rich, famous, or talented. It wasn't just because she was beautiful. It wasn't just because she had the capability of leading, inspiring, and commanding a room full of tens of thousands of people.

All those things were true, but that wasn't why he loved her. He loved her nature, her spirit, and her heart. He loved her when she was sick and when she was well. And the best part of it all was that he could tell she loved him in that same way. He could tell she loved him in spite of his struggles and his past mistakes. She loved him for who he was.

There was still so much to do in their relationship—so much to talk about and so many steps to make. No one besides Daniel and Courtney really knew the extent of the feelings they had for each other. She hadn't even met his family, and they hadn't even been seen in public together.

But none of that mattered.

Daniel knew that everything would fall into place. What mattered most was that love existed at the very core of their budding relationship. At the center of it was true love—the type of love that no one could take away from them—the type of love that didn't see outward beauty, or talent, or past failures.

It was that spark that drove Daniel to take real, practical steps in overcoming his past. It was that spark that caused him to get on yet another plane and go to Los Angeles.

He found himself at a farewell party for the road crew of Courtney's Freedom Tour. He knew the road was physically taxing on her and that this would be her last tour for a while, if not for good. She hadn't made any official announcements, but Daniel knew she was more than ready for an extended break.

He watched her at the party, thinking he could understand why. He had seen her in action backstage when he was filling in for Trevor, but he was so preoccupied with making sure he had security under control that he wasn't able to fully appreciate how very much of herself she poured into leading this group. He didn't fully grasp it until that night at the party.

He watched as Courtney captured the love and attention of her team and their guests. There was a dinner followed by an awards ceremony with trophies and gifts for the whole crew. Courtney made a touching speech about how special each of them were and how the tour wouldn't have been a success without their hard work and dedication. She was truly humble and grateful, yet at the same time, she was a strong, passionate leader.

Daniel was already in love with her before this evening ever happened, but seeing her in action with the crew put him over the top. He was so proud of her.

She finished her speech and wished them all the best, and then he watched in amazement as a couple of the tables in the back of the room began to chant.

"Freedom!

Hoo.

Freedom!

Hoo.

Freedom!

Hoo."

They shouted the word 'freedom' as a war cry, and then the word 'hoo' was said in a low, guttural tone like a bass drum, keeping the rhythm between each cry. They all stomped when they called out, making it even more dramatic.

It was a chant Courtney led backstage before every show to pump everyone up. She usually got it started, but this time the chant began in the back of the room.

Before long, the whole room was swaying side to side with the rhythm. Courtney smiled and shook her head at the fact that they wanted one last song. She put the mic to her mouth and made a confident pose like she was a rock star from way back.

"We got some cameras.
Hoo.
We got some lights.
Hoo.
We got our costumes.
Hoo.
We lookin' tight.
Hoo.
We got our dancers.
Hoo.
We got our band.
Hoo.
We got a room.
Hoo.
Sold out with fans.
Hoo.
They out there now.

Hoo.
All goin' crazy.
Hoo.
Cause they all know.
Hoo.
This show's amazing."

Daniel had seen her do that chant before, but there were a lot of people in the room who had never been present to witness it, and he watched in amazement as everyone in the room got pumped up in spite of there being no crowd waiting or show to perform.

Everyone burst into applause when they finished, and Courtney blew kisses and yelled, "I love you guys!"

"We love you Courtney!" someone yelled through the applause.

She bowed and then held her hands out as if offering them all a big hug. Her arms were still extended as she opened her hand and let the microphone drop, causing them all to yell out again.

***

"I can't believe they started the chant," Trevor said in the limo on the way home.

"I know," Gabe said. "That was crazy. That was my favorite part of the whole night—besides the steak. Did you practice that?"

"She does it with them before every show," Denise said.

"She changes it up some," Trevor said. "Sometimes she mentions the name of the town or calls out specific people, but it's similar to that every time."

"Those awards were funny too," Gabe said.

They talked about it the whole way to Courtney's house. Daniel chimed in a little, but Gabe, Denise, and Trevor were so excited that he and Courtney just let them chatter.

For the last couple of hours Courtney had given herself over to leading her team just like she did when they were on the road, so she was glad for the opportunity to be quiet. She held Daniel by the arm, resting her head on his shoulder. She noticed when they were pulling up in her driveway, and she leaned up to speak near Daniel's ear.

"Are you staying at my house?" she asked.

He turned and gave her a little smile. "Are you giving me the option not to?"

"Not really," she said. "I mean, if you really don't want to stay, then I'm not going to—" she stopped talking when Daniel leaned down to speak next to her ear.

She was sweet and tender, and she smelled like heaven to him. "Courtney," he whispered. "I really don't want to leave your side."

Daniel's words made her squeeze his arm tightly, which caused all sorts of protective, desirous feelings to course through his body. He had to have her in his life and that's all there was to it. He would work it out with his brother, or his own feelings, or whatever else he thought might get in the way. She held onto him tightly, and he realized that he wouldn't let anything get in the way.

"My things are at the hotel," he said.

Denise overheard his statement, and she chimed in. "I can send for someone to pick up your stuff if you want," she said.

"Would you, please," Courtney said.

"You staying with us?" Trevor asked.

"Of course he is," Courtney said. "I have tons of room."

Daniel knew Trevor lived at Courtney's house. His full-time protection was part of the job, and ultimately, Daniel took comfort in that, but he couldn't help but cringe when Trevor said the word 'us'. He was considering his own jealousy when the limo driver came around to open the door for them.

Trevor got out first, leaving the two couples in the backseat. "Are you guys coming in?" Courtney asked.

Denise looked at Gabe who shrugged as if it was up to her.

"We can go swimming," Courtney added.

Denise raised her eyebrows at Gabe and then looked at Courtney. "I'd have to borrow a bathing suit," she said.

"So would I, actually," Gabe said.

"Me too," Daniel added.

"I have one for you, Denise, and I'm sure Trevor's got something in there for the boys. Whata ya say?"

"I'm game," Denise said with a shrug.

By the time the couples made it into the house, Trevor had already checked things out and was standing in the kitchen chewing a bite of food.

"We're gonna swim," Courtney announced. "The boys will need to borrow some of your swim trunks if you don't mind."

"Not at all," Trevor said.

"I'm going to take care of getting your things picked up from the hotel," Denise said to Daniel. "What's your room number again?"

"604," Daniel said. "Are you sure it's not a problem? I can go get it myself."

Denise shook her head. "I'll just ask the concierge to get it packed up and send the driver back over there. Let me catch him before he leaves."

Denise took out her phone and began pushing buttons, and Courtney took her by the arm pulling her toward the bedroom.

"You can do that while we change," Courtney said. She looked at Daniel. "Trevor will hook you up with a pair of shorts," she said with a smile.

It was fifteen minutes later when Courtney and Denise finished changing into their swimsuits and making all of the arrangements to get Daniel's things brought over. Of course, they talked while they were doing that. Denise was a wonderful assistant who knew how to maintain professional boundaries, so she never asked Courtney too many questions about her personal life or feelings. Courtney wasn't much of a gabber, and Denise respected that. She was, however, curious about Daniel because she could see how very affected Courtney was by him. She asked Courtney if she planned on being seen in public with Daniel, and Courtney told her that she was more than ready to go public with their relationship and was only taking it slow out of respect for Daniel.

Daniel and Gabe were waiting in the kitchen for the girls when they came downstairs. Daniel had borrowed a pair of Trevor's swim trunks that were a blue and white striped pattern. He had been wearing an undershirt under his tux, and he left it on when he changed.

Gabe hadn't done the same. He was shirtless, but Daniel felt more comfortable leaving a shirt on until they got into the pool. Courtney and Denise were both wearing swimsuits when they came downstairs, but Daniel only had eyes for one of them. She was wearing a blue one-piece number with gold accents, and she came into the kitchen smiling at him and looking like she belonged on the cover of Sports Illustrated.

"Where's Trevor?" Courtney asked.

"In his room," Daniel said. "He said he might meet us out there in a little while."

Courtney nodded as she came to stand right in front of Daniel. She looked straight at him, causing him to experience that same wave of protective desire he always seemed to get with her.

"We'll meet you guys out there," Courtney said, talking to Denise and Gabe but looking straight at Daniel.

The other two took off for the swimming pool, leaving Courtney and Daniel in the kitchen. "I'm pretty sure Gabe and Trevor couldn't care less about looking at me, but I still wore a one-piece for you," Courtney said.

Daniel scanned her body from head to toe before making eye contact with her again. "I'm pretty sure no one can really care less about looking at you, Courtney, so I'm glad about the one-piece. Thank you."

"I'm not glad about *your* one-piece," she said, looking him over the same way he had done to her.

"I was thinking about taking my shirt off before we got in the pool," he said, touching his stomach.

"*Thinking* about it?" She asked incredulously. "I wouldn't have even suggested a swim if I would've known you were a shirt-swimmer."

He laughed at that.

Courtney didn't have to see him without a shirt. She could see the shape of his chest through this thin undershirt and knew she was going to be in trouble once he took it off.

Daniel, on the other hand, was already in trouble. He wasn't lying when he said Courtney would look beautiful in a canvas sack, and there she was in a gorgeous blue swimsuit, staring at him like he hung the moon.

Chapter 15
Courtney
Memphis, TN

It had been almost a month since Daniel surprised me by coming to California. He stayed for five days, and before he left, we made plans to see each other again the following month when I would travel to Memphis for his little sister's graduation.

When we made the arrangements, I thought I would be so busy that a month would fly by, but I was wrong. I had been busy, but that didn't change the fact that I went to bed every night wishing I had seen Daniel that day and counting the minutes until I finally got to.

Trevor flew to Memphis with me once it finally came time for my trip. The plan was that he would escort me there and then fly to his hometown of Buffalo, New York where he would take a well-deserved vacation.

I was planning on staying in Memphis for two weeks, and already I was dreading the time when my trip would be over and I would again have to say goodbye to Daniel. I had talked to his little sister, Ivy, on the phone a time or two during the last month, but she had no idea that I was coming to town or that I was planning on going to her graduation.

Daniel was close to his family and I knew they were aware that something was going on between us, but I didn't know exactly how much he had told them. The media hadn't found out about us either. This was one of the only bonuses of our relationship being long-distance. I was glad for Daniel that we had taken things slow, but I was more than ready for everyone to know about us, and I hoped the paparazzi would catch wind of me going to Memphis so that we could be photographed together.

"Don't be nervous," Trevor said as he handed me the bag he took out of the overhead compartment.

"How do you know I'm nervous?" I asked.

"You picked at your fingernails during the whole flight."

"I did?" I glanced down at my own hand realizing that he was right. My fingernails were all really short.

"You shouldn't be nervous," Trevor continued. "The Bishops are wonderful people, and they're really going to love you."

"You think?" I asked as we started to exit the plane.

"Who wouldn't?" he asked.

We paused our conversation to respond to the flight attendant who was thanking us as we walked off of the plane.

Trevor and I were professionals at navigating airports together, and we stuck right by each other all the way through the terminal toward baggage claim. I knew Daniel would be waiting there for me, and I got more and more antsy the closer we got. I heard a couple of people whisper my name while we were walking, but I had on glasses and my fake, curly hairpiece so I just pretended not to hear them.

Denise was a master at planning my travel arrangements, and I knew I wouldn't have to wait for my bag to come around on the carousel. There would, no doubt, be an attendant standing by to deliver it to me.

Normally, Trevor and I would find the person who was holding our bags and make our way over to them before scooting out of the airport. This time, I didn't care about my bags. This time, I was only looking for one person, and that was Daniel Bishop.

I had already begun scanning the room when we were halfway down the escalator.

"There's Daniel," Trevor said, seeing him first.

"Where?"

He pointed, and I glanced in that direction to find Daniel standing twenty or thirty feet from the bottom of the escalator. He had on a baseball cap, which was why it took me a second to find him. It was the first time I had ever seen him wearing one of those, and I smiled at how handsome he looked in it. He smiled back at me, and I could see his perfect white teeth even though there was what seemed like a crazy, unreasonable distance between us.

He had on dark jeans and a baby blue T-shirt, and I was so excited to see him that I unintentionally began bouncing up and down in this shaky, jerky motion. There were people in front of us on the escalator, and I felt like I wanted to hurl my body over them so that I could get to Daniel quicker.

"Oh my gosh," Trevor said, teasing me. "You better calm down, or he's going to think you like him."

I smiled and squinted at Trevor.

"I see your bags," he said, nudging his chin in the direction of the baggage carousel. "I'll go get them for you and meet you guys in a minute."

"Thank you," I said.

I grabbed his hand and gave it a little squeeze before stepping off of the escalator.

I ran into Daniel.

I hadn't planned on doing that, but there was nothing I could do to stop myself once my feet hit the ground. Thankfully, he came toward me as well, and we closed the distance in no time at all. He caught me in his arms, literally sweeping me off my feet. Both of us had on baseball caps, and our faces came so close together that the bills got in the way. Daniel held me in mid-air with one arm around my waist while he took the other hand and swiftly switched his hat so that it was facing backwards. He smiled when he got it into position and then proceeded to place excited kisses all over the side of my face and neck. I giggled as he did that and then set me back on my feet. I kept my arms wrapped around his neck, stretching upward to remain as close to him as possible.

"I misssssssed yooooouuuu," I moaned in his ear before placing several kisses on his neck.

"I missed you too," he said. He leaned to the side so that he could avoid my cap when he ducked to put a quick kiss right my lips.

"That was the longest month ever," I said, wrinkling my nose at him as I grabbed the sides of his gorgeous face.

I flexed my hands, letting my fingertips rub his cheeks. He looked like he hadn't shaved in a couple of weeks, and the short stubble was now long enough to feel soft to the touch.

"You got some fuzz," I said.

"Whatcha think?" he asked, grabbing his own jaw.

"I think it's so handsome."

Trevor came to stand next to us with my bags. "You guys have an audience, just so you know," he said discreetly. "A few people are taking pictures over there. I didn't know if you were planning on standing here and being in love all day or what."

I smiled at Trevor and let go of Daniel so that I could hug him. "You're the best," I said. "Thank you for getting my bags."

"You're welcome," Trevor said, hugging me back. "I'm glad you're in good hands." He reached out to give Daniel a guy-hug with a hearty slap on the back.

"I hope you have a great time with your family," I said.

"Yeah, enjoy your vacation," Daniel said.

Trevor smiled. "I will. Tell Gray and the rest of the gang 'hi' for me. I'll see you both in a couple of weeks."

Trevor waved to us and then turned to head back into the terminal so that he could catch his next flight. I saw a group of people standing near the baggage claim who were staring at me and whispering and pointing like they were working up the nerve to approach me. I loved and appreciated my fans, but I knew from past experiences that moments like these could easily turn chaotic. Daniel saw my expression shift and he grabbed my bags in one hand and wrapped his other arm around my shoulder, urging me toward the door.

"I've got someone out here for you to meet," he said as we made our way outside. "I hope you don't mind."

"Who is it?" I asked.

We had already stepped out onto the curb by the time I got the question out of my mouth, and Daniel gestured to a truck that was parked right in front of us. The driver smiled and leaned over to open the door, and my heart began pounding because instantly, I realized who it was. He was so ruggedly handsome that I hardly noticed the scar that ran down the right side of his face. Owen.

"This is my brother, Owen," Daniel said, opening the door more fully so that I could climb in. I stepped into the truck while Daniel went to work putting my bags into the back of it.

"You must be Courtney," Owen said, smiling and reaching out to shake my hand once I was settled into the seat next to him. I went to shake his hand but changed my mind and instead went straight for a hug. He let out a little laugh at the impromptu change of plans, but he easily went with it and seemed thankful that I was content to skip the formalities. He smelled a little like his brother and I smiled, thinking that all the Bishop boys must smell good.

"I'm sweaty, sorry," he said after we hugged.

I giggled. "I was just thinking that you smelled good."

He let out a little laugh. "You must like the smell of motorcycles. I'm just getting off work."

I was so nervous that I didn't know what to say next. I wanted to say something about his scar being handsome, but I knew that would just be putting my foot in my mouth, so I kept quiet. Thankfully, Daniel climbed into the truck, offering some distraction.

"Owen offered to take your bags to my house," Daniel said. "He'll drop them off for you. It might be a few of hours before we get back there, so if you need to get anything out of them you should probably go ahead and get it now."

"Where are we going?" I asked.

"You'll see," Daniel said.

Rather than exiting the airport, Owen made a circle and got in the lane that was marked 'short-term parking'.

"Where are we going?" I asked again.

"I knew you would have bags with you, so I couldn't pick you up on it," Daniel said.

He pointed out the front window of the truck, and my heart dropped. In the distance, on the far side of the parking garage, I saw a motorcycle. It was a simple, matte black two-seater. It was clean and shiny, and it looked like it had just been driven off of the showroom floor.

Owen pulled up and parked right next to it, and I leaned over Daniel so that I could get a good look. It was the most beautiful motorcycle I had ever seen. It was perfect and simple, and it looked like it had been made just for Daniel. There was a silver emblem on the gas tank that said *Bishop Motorcycles*, and my heart swelled with pride when it sank in that his family had made that thing.

"Is that yours?" I asked with wide eyes.

Daniel nodded. I was tempted to mention the fact that I thought he didn't ride, but again, I thought better of it in present company.

"Are we going to ride it?" I asked instead.

Daniel smiled and nodded at me as he opened the passenger's door. We climbed out, and Daniel held the door open so that he could talk to his brother. I instantly started inspecting the motorcycle and imagining myself riding on the back of it. I wasn't nervous about it at all. I absolutely couldn't wait. There was nothing I could do to stop a huge smile from spreading across my face.

Daniel had been standing there saying something to his brother while I was preoccupied with checking out the bike, but I came up next to him, staring at him with excitement.

"Are we really getting on this?" I asked.

He smiled and nodded, pulling me close by wrapping his hand around my back. It gave me chills.

"Right now?" I asked.

His smile broadened. "Right now." He reached out and slapped the top of his brother's truck. "Just leave her bags in my living room, if you don't mind," he said. "We'll meet you at Mom's in an hour or so."

Owen nodded, and Daniel started to close the door, but he hesitated.

"Don't tell Ivy," he added. "She doesn't know Courtney's here. I want to surprise her."

Owen smiled and waved as Daniel closed the door.

"It was so nice to meet you!" I called as the door closed. I cringed, knowing Owen only heard about half of my sentence, but he rolled down the window, smiling at me.

"It was great to meet you too, Courtney," he said. "I'll see you over at the house when you're done with your ride. Y'all have fun."

Chapter 16

Owen backed out of his parking spot and drove off, leaving Daniel and me standing next to the black motorcycle. I was so overwhelmed that I didn't even know where to begin. I wanted to say about five different things at once. I gawked at him as I absentmindedly pointed in the direction of Owen as he drove away.

"That was Owen," I said.

Daniel grinned and nodded at me.

"He's so handsome."

"He's a Bishop," Daniel said with an irresistibly confident smile and shrug.

I couldn't resist—I reached up and wrapped my arms around his neck. "I missed you so much," I said.

"How much?" he asked, pulling me close.

"The most," I answered.

"I missed you at least that much," he said.

I cut my eyes toward the beautiful motorcycle that was parked next to us.

"Don't worry," he said. "I've been practicing."

I made a disbelieving face. "I'm not worried," I said. "I'm excited. I can't wait."

He grinned. "Are you ready, then?"

My face lit up as an answer to his question, and he smiled as he let go of me and walked over to the bike. I followed and stood by his side, watching as he stepped over the seat, straddling the bike. He seemed totally comfortable and confident, and I started to get on, but he said, "Let me get it started first, and then you can get on."

He had two helmets hanging from the handlebars, and he put one on and made me do the same. There was a little leather pouch on the side of the motorcycle, and he stashed our caps inside.

"I'm gonna start it now," he warned.

I took a step back and watched as Daniel started the engine. It revved to life with a loud, low rumble that startled me and made me giggle. Daniel grinned at the site of my reaction and then he motioned with a flick of his head for me to get on. He held the bike steady while I stepped on it and then he turned and explained what parts of the bike would be hot and that I should avoid touching them. He also explained that I should hold on tightly to his waist, which was an absolute pleasure, obviously.

"You ready?" he yelled over his shoulder. I could feel his stomach flinch when he called to me, and I closed my eyes, feeling way too giddy.

"Yes!" I said.

And without another word, Daniel took off.

He drove slowly since we were in a parking garage, but it was still such a thrill. I had never been on the back of a motorcycle, and the feeling of him balancing it underneath me was exhilarating. The low sound of the engine echoed in the parking garage, and I smiled when we got to the exit and he started going faster.

There wasn't a whole lot of traffic at the airport, and soon we were on city streets. I marveled at how different the atmosphere felt when riding a motorcycle rather than driving a car. Memphis was different than L.A., but it wasn't just that. I felt almost naked, like everyone was looking at us, which they sort of were.

I wasn't sure how long we had ridden, maybe 10 minutes or so, before we got out of the city and into the countryside. Daniel was a careful driver, but he drove fast enough that the wind whipped all around me, almost taking my breath away. I couldn't stop smiling. I was smiling so much that my cheeks would, no doubt, be sore from it.

Daniel drove into the woods. It was late afternoon, and the cover of trees made it even darker than it already was. The roads began to wind and bend as we climbed a hillside, and I breathed in the crisp, woodsy smell of the forest.

Finally, after we had driven some ways into the woods, Daniel found a landing near the side of the road and pulled off onto it. He stopped the bike, killed the engine, and put down the kickstand before looking over his shoulder at me. I stretched up and placed a kiss on his cheek causing our helmets to touch. This made him take his helmet off, and I did the same. He hung them from the handlebars before turning to face me again.

156

"Come here," he said. He swiveled at the waist to take hold of me.

"Come where?"

"Up here."

He held the bike steady with his legs while using his arms to lead me where he wanted me to go. I wound up in the driver's seat. He scooted back, taking my old seat and letting me have his. He positioned me on the front of the bike where I was facing him instead of the road. My legs laid over his—our thighs crossing each other. It was glorious. I reached out and grabbed one of his hands, bringing it up and placing it palm-down on my chest.

"This is how I feel right now," I said, referring to my pounding heart.

"Because of riding a motorcycle?" he asked.

"And because of my driver," I said.

He looked at me like he was checking me out, and I felt nervous because of it. I had been wearing a hat and the hairpiece followed by a helmet, so I was relatively sure my hair was in disarray. I ran my hand through it, shaking it out before focusing on him again.

"You're amazing," he said. "It's hard for me to believe you're on the front of my bike right now. You're like something a man would dream-up in his wildest fantasy."

"What about *this* man?" I asked, pointing at his chest.

He caught my hand, staring at me and lifting an eyebrow like he was a predator who had me in his trap. "I don't have to dream you up," he said. "I've got you right here."

I was so in love with him, so blown away by my current situation on the front of his bike, that my heart absolutely rattled in my chest. I was so stirred up that I had to make an effort to stop my teeth from clacking together. I bit my lip.

"You okay?" he asked sweetly.

"So okay," I said. I touched the side of his face. I was in absolute awe. "I don't know if I've ever been so okay, honestly, Daniel."

He touched the side of my face with his finger as he stared at me. "I don't know if I've ever been so okay either, Courtney."

We leaned toward each other, letting our faces get closer and closer. We moved at a torturously slow pace, closing the distance a millimeter at a time as we gazed into each other's eyes. I could barely breathe. Slowly, slowly, ever so slowly, we let our faces come closer together until we were only an inch or two apart. My lungs were barely functioning. I realized that Daniel and I were so close that we were sharing the same breath. His gorgeous, full lips were so miraculously close to mine that I could literally feel him breathing. We stayed there, letting our breath mingle and enjoying the beautiful, torturous moment for several long heartbeats.

"I think I love you," I whispered as I stared into his dark eyes.

The corner of his mouth turned upward into a slow grin. I was looking directly into his eyes, but I could see his cheeks move and knew that he was smiling at me.

"Me too," he said.

"You what?" I asked.

"Love you."

"Say it to me," I whispered.

"I love you, Courtney."

Our mouths were so close that he nearly brushed up against me when he spoke. This caused a feeling of warmth to spread inside me and I squeezed his hand.

"You do?" I whispered.

"Uh-huh."

"Enough to introduce me to your family?"

"Yep."

"Enough to take me on a motorcycle ride?"

"Yep."

"What else?" I asked.

"Anything you want."

"Enough to kiss me?"

"Uh-huh," he said.

"Really?"

He nodded.

"I heard I was your first kiss," I said.

"You were," he said. "And my second."

"And your third, and eighth, and all the way up to forever?" I asked hopefully.

"I think so," he said with a little smirk.

"Good," I whispered.

We stayed in that same position for a few more seconds until it was just too much temptation for me. I leaned forward, letting our mouths finally make contact. I reached up and grabbed his face, holding him securely as I let my lips softly and gently mold to his. I kissed him over and over again—all soft, tender kisses that reflected how genuinely relieved I was to see him. I didn't realize I had begun leaning into him until I broke the kiss and realized that our bodies were pressed against each other. Daniel was holding me by the waist like he never planned on letting me go. Our faces were still only about an inch apart, and he smiled at me and glanced around at our surroundings.

"We better get going," he said. "My mom is expecting us for dinner."

I pulled back and ran my hands through my hair, putting it in a ponytail with the hairband that was wrapped around my wrist. "How am I supposed to meet your family looking like this?"

"You mean looking like a gorgeous, flawless, famous rock star?" he asked, teasing me.

I playfully scrunched my face at him before getting off of the seat, and he helped me steady myself next to the bike. I turned and glanced at my reflection in the rearview mirror. There was nothing rock star about how I looked after a plane ride, a motorcycle ride, and a kiss, but I didn't have anything between my teeth or sticking out of my nose, so it would have to do.

"Who's all gonna be there?" I asked.

"Ivy's the only one of us who still lives at home. I expect her to be home, but I'm not sure because I didn't tell her you were coming. My mom and dad will be there for sure, and Owen. I wanted you to meet Aunt Jane and Uncle Gray, but they're in Nashville for the weekend. The whole family would've come if I would have told them, but that could amount to about fifteen or twenty people, and I didn't know if you would be up for that on day one."

"I want to meet them all," I said. "But I'm happy to get to see your parents first—and Ivy and Owen."

I put on my helmet and Daniel did the same before I stepped back to let him start the engine. I was definitely not graceful at getting onto the bike, but he held it securely and made it as easy as possible for me.

He turned the motorcycle around and we headed back the way we came—through the woods and down a long country road before we entered Memphis again. We drove through a section of the city before entering a nice neighborhood where all of the houses were set back off the road with huge yards and lots of trees. He drove slowly and pointed at one house as we passed it.

"My grandparents live right there," he said, yelling over his shoulder.

"Michael and Ivy?" I asked, making sure I had their names straight.

"Yeah. It looks like they're home, but I'm not gonna stop right now. You'll meet them soon."

I stared at the house as we passed. I couldn't see much of it from the road, but I could tell it was a gorgeous brick home with tons of charm. We hadn't even gone another mile down the road before Daniel pulled into a long driveway. There was a beautiful, light-colored wooden house at the end of it, and my heart started beating like crazy when I realized his family was waiting inside. I squeezed him and leaned up to speak near his ear.

"Is this it?" I asked even though I knew the answer to my question.

He turned to look at me from over his shoulder with a nod. "This is where I grew up," he said. "Do you like it?"

"I love it," I said.

Chapter 17

"Ivy's not here," Daniel said once he parked the motorcycle and killed the engine.

We had driven around to the back of the house so Daniel could park by the garage. The garage doors were open, and he gestured inside, indicating that the empty spot was how he knew Ivy wasn't home. I glanced at the vehicles that were parked inside—a truck and a SUV along with at least four motorcycles. Owen's truck was also there, but it was parked outside.

I was so nervous about meeting his parents that I could hardly breathe. I smiled, trying to pretend I was calm. I handed Daniel my helmet, and he hung it from the handlebar along with his before getting off of the motorcycle.

"Who all's here?" I asked, unable to hide my anticipation.

"It looks like it's just Owen and my parents." He took me by the hand and began pulling me inside through the garage.

"We're going in this way?" I asked.

I was somewhat surprised that he wanted to hold my hand, but I was thankful for it, and I held onto him tightly.

"We go in through the garage most of the time," he said as we walked. He pointed at the door leading to the house. "This leads to a mudroom and then into the kitchen," he said, glancing at me.

I gave him a thankful smile for the explanation. Daniel could see that I was nervous, and he stopped in front of the door and used his finger to tilt my chin so that I would look at him.

"They're going to love you," he said. "And you're gonna love them."

"I'm pretty picky," I said, joking.

Daniel grinned as he opened the door, heading inside. His description was accurate. We passed through a hallway that had a mudroom feel to it and was attached to a laundry room. We kept going until we reached the kitchen. It was bigger than I expected, opening up into a grand living room. I could see Owen standing in the living room with another man, but both of them were facing the television, which was switched to a baseball game.

"Oh my goodness, I didn't even hear y'all pull up!" a woman's voice called.

I glanced toward the right side of the living room to see a beautiful woman heading in our direction wearing a huge smile. There were two huge rooms separating us and she already had her arms outstretched like she was coming in for a hug.

"I saw them pull up, but I didn't hear them come in," said the man who I assumed was Daniel's dad as he turned to smile at us. "I thought they were still outside."

All three of them came our way, wearing welcoming smiles as we met in the kitchen.

"Mr. and Mrs. Bishop, I assume." I said the words as she reached out to hug me tightly.

"Rose, baby, please," she said.

"And Jesse," his dad said, hugging me once his mom let me go.

"Owen said you met at the airport," Rose said, motioning to her son.

I nodded, and gave Owen a slight bow, but he reached out to hug me as well, so I returned it gratefully. "Good to see you again," I said.

He smiled. "I brought your bags to Daniel's."

"Thank you," I said. "I really enjoyed taking a ride. I've never done that before."

"Pretty fun, huh?" Rose said with a big smile as she cozied up next to her husband.

"I can't believe you guys built that thing. It's so neat seeing your last name written on it."

"You'll have to come by the shop," Owen said.

"I've actually been to a Bishop dealership in L.A. I've just never ridden one."

"When'd you go to a Bishop dealership?" Daniel asked, glancing at me curiously.

"I made Trevor take me a couple weeks ago," I said. "I was curious and wanted to see what it was all about. We didn't ride one or anything; I just looked around."

"The L.A. store's nice, but we have the original factory and dealership in Memphis," Owen said. "It's our biggest location and we have the original garage… the only one with Elvis."

I gave him a perplexed look, and he smiled.

"A parrot," Rose explained. "He's like 50 years old, and he's been hanging out at the garage, squawking at people since it first opened."

"Yeah, the dealership in L.A. definitely didn't have an Elvis," I said.

"It had a portrait of him," Jesse said. "They all do. It's part of the décor that goes into all the branches—a big ole' painting of Elvis, standing on his perch."

I laughed. "That's hilarious," I said. "I really wish I would have noticed that."

"You can come meet the real Elvis," Owen said. "And then, when you go back to Los Angeles, you'll be able to tell them you saw him in person."

Owen didn't mean anything by mentioning that I would go back to Los Angeles, but the statement still made my heart sink. I smiled and nodded, pretending to be unfazed.

"I'll definitely have to look for that," I said.

"Where's Ivy?" Daniel asked.

Jesse shook his head. "Your mother told her to be home for dinner, but you never know with that girl. She'll probably show up at 8:30 and say she was just getting hungry."

"She would've been here by now if you would've let me tell her you were bringing Courtney," Rose said. "And speaking of dinner, it's ready if you guys are hungry." Rose broke away from her husband and headed toward the kitchen.

"I am," Daniel said.

"Me too," Owen added as he started to walk over there.

"It smells really good," I said.

Rose had made a gorgeous meal, which included lasagna, salad, and bread sticks, and we sat around the table laughing and talking and getting to know each other as we ate. They asked questions about my job, and I asked questions about theirs. We talked about the other members of the family, including Wes who was in London and Jesse's sister, Jane, who lived close by and had two children that were roughly Daniel's age. I told them that I had met Shelby years before, and they all got a kick out of that.

Daniel had already given me lots of details about his extended family, but it was fun to hear everyone else talk about them, and I felt happy that they wanted to share that sort of stuff with me. I gave them a brief history of my life, saying that I was an only child and telling them how I got started in show business. We talked about Jesse's mom being a singer, and Jesse told a couple of stories from when he was a kid and she used to take him and his sister on tour with her.

We sat at the dinner table for a long time before the guys excused themselves to go into the living room so that they could catch up on the baseball game. Rose said she had been meaning to water the ferns on the front porch, and she invited me to join her. Daniel told her I might be more comfortable staying inside with him, but I opted to go outside with his mother just because I liked her and wanted to.

She crossed to the far side of the porch and sat down on the swing, patting the seat next to her and inviting me to sit down.

"I don't really need to water the ferns," she said. "I just did that yesterday. I brought you out here to talk to you for a minute."

"Sure," I said. I smiled at her, but I was suddenly anxious and wondered what she had to say.

I sat beside her, and she put her hand on my leg before turning to stare at me earnestly. She took a slow, deep breath and her eyes filled with tears, instantly causing tears to rise to my own eyes. She regarded me sincerely and cleared her throat, trying her best to get herself together so she could say what she wanted to say.

"A couple of months ago, Daniel went to Florida with Ivy and me for a gymnastics tournament," she said.

She spoke slowly and deliberately and had to clear her throat every time she paused. I could see by the slight quiver of her chin that she was trying not to break down and cry, and I felt moved to reach out and hold her hand. She received my touch gratefully and offered me a sweet smile. She was beautiful, and

I could see elements of Daniel in her. She took another deep breath before continuing.

"As you know, while we were down in Florida, Daniel got a call to fill-in on a job."

I nodded.

"Well, he traveled with you to New Orleans after that. He was only gone for a few days, but when he came home, I could tell something had shifted in him. Something was a little bit different. He was acting upset, but I could tell it was because he was happy, if that makes any sense."

I nodded.

She let out another long sigh, looking at me like she regretted something.

"I should probably back up a little bit and tell you that I haven't seen my son happy in quite some time."

Her face crumpled and tears fell onto her cheeks when she made that statement. She covered her face with her hands. I had no other choice but to reach out and hug her. We sat on the swing, holding each other close for a few seconds before she wiped her face and continued.

"So, then a few days after he got back from doing that job, he surprised us all by hopping on a plane to go to Dallas," she said. "And when he got home from that that trip, he came over to the house and he asked…"

She trailed off, unable to finish her sentence. I pulled back to look at her and saw that her face was contorted with tears.

"I'm so sorry," she said, shaking her head and covering her face.

"Don't be," I whispered.

Tears were gathering in my own eyes as well, so I blinked as I stared at her, waiting for her to continue.

"He came over the night he came back from Dallas, and he told his dad he wanted to learn how to ride a... to ride a motorcycle."

She paused and shook her head, gasping for air between sobs.

"I'm sorry," she repeated. "It's just been such a long road for Daniel. As a mom... (sniff) it's so hard to see your baby suffer. I really apologize. I told myself I was going to do this without crying. I just meant to bring you out here and thank you."

She wiped at her tears, smiling at herself for being unable to stop them.

"He's been at it for weeks," she said. "He started by himself, going out with his dad, and then, (sniff) one day he came over and asked if I'd get on the back and... (sniff) go for a ride with him..."

She put her face in her hands, letting out a long, wheezing sob, and I rubbed her back as tears flowed from my own eyes.

"I didn't mean to cry. I just wanted to thank you. I know it might not seem like a big deal that he wanted to get on a bike again, but to us it is. To us, it's a very big deal. It's not that motorcycles mean that much to us, or anything… it's not about that. It's something deeper than that. It was like his heart was healing."

We hugged each other for what must have been a full minute as we both wiped our eyes and got ourselves together. About halfway through the silence, she nudged the ground with her foot, causing us to start swinging.

"Daniel has changed things for me, too," I said, finally. "Not in the same way, but he brought healing into my life, too. Not just physically, either, although that's part of it. He honestly helped me see a side of God that I didn't know existed—he helped me know that there's a God out there who loves me—a God I wanted to get to know."

"Oh my goodness," Rose said with a thoughtful sigh. She rubbed my leg. "That's so special, baby. Thank you for sharing that with me."

After a moment, a car pulled into the driveway.

"That's Ivy," Rose explained when she glanced that way.

I started to ask if we should go inside, but I was still teary-eyed and really comfortable sitting on the swing with Daniel's mom, so I just stayed there. Neither of us moved. We sat, comfortably leaning against each other and swinging gently.

About three minutes had passed when the front door flew open, and a stunned Ivy Bishop stepped onto the porch, staring at us.

I giggled at the intensity of her facial expression.

"I can't believe you came to my house for dinner and nobody told me!" she said, staring straight at me.

She grinned and shook her head and she started to walk toward us, and her face shifted to a look of confusion when she was about halfway across the porch. "Are y'all bawling?"

Chapter 18

"I was just telling Courtney how remarkable it was that Daniel wanted to ride again," Rose explained.

Ivy smiled and breathed a sigh, shaking her head. "Yeah, it seems like every other day he's asking me to go for a ride with him," she said. "I thought he was just obsessed with having somebody on the back of his new bike. I didn't know he was practicing for someone."

"I knew he was practicing," Rose said. "I put the pieces together the second he told your dad he wanted to ride again."

"It makes total sense now," Ivy said.

She hugged me as we scooted over so that she could take a seat on the swing next to us. It was a big porch swing and there was plenty of room for the three of us. I ended up in the middle, which felt great. For years, I had been surrounded by people who loved me and were excited to be around me, but those relationships always felt like they hinged on my music. These women just wanted to sit next to me on a porch swing and talk about the fact that Daniel finally wanted to ride a motorcycle again.

"When'd you get here?" Ivy said.

"To Memphis or your mom's house?" I asked.

"Both."

"Today. Just a few hours ago," I said. "Daniel picked me up at the airport and we went for a drive before coming here to eat dinner. Your mom made lasagna and salad."

Ivy leaned forward and looked past me at her mom with a narrow-eyed expression that made me laugh.

"Your father told you to be home for dinner," Rose said innocently.

"I was helping Shelby hang pictures and stuff," Ivy said. "She said we could have a party at her house after graduation."

"Shelby just bought her first house," Rose said, looking at me. Then she leveled her daughter with a stern, motherly look. "And y'all better not be planning anything wild over there. I know she wouldn't appreciate that."

"We're not, Mom," Ivy said before looking at me. "I'm graduating next week," she said. "That's what the party's for. A bunch of my friends from school are coming."

I smiled. "I was telling your parents that I met Shelby before," I said. "We were both really young. She might not even remember."

"She remembers," Ivy said, nodding. "I told her about meeting you in Miami, and she told me how y'all met when you were kids. How long are you gonna be in town? You could see her if you come to the party."

174

Ivy was half-joking when she made that last comment, but I shrugged like it might be a possibility.

"I'm definitely planning on coming to your graduation," I said. "Daniel invited me. That's one of the main reasons I planned my trip for this week."

I had to laugh at Ivy's reaction. She tried not to get too excited, but her legs straightened out and she began stiffly paddling her feet in tiny, quick up-and-down motions like she was swimming in a pool.

"Are you staying a whole week?"

I nodded.

"Don't worry," she said, still kicking. "I'm not going to go around telling people you're here or anything. I know I'd have the whole town trying to come over to my house."

The front door opened, and Daniel stepped onto the porch staring into the front yard with an intense expression. He squinted into the distance, looking toward the road.

"What's the matter, Daniel?" Rose asked.

"Nothing," Daniel said. "But why don't you ladies go ahead and come in for now?"

The three of us stood from the porch swing and made our way into the house. Daniel held the door open for us, but he and I hung back in the doorway so that I could talk to him and ask what was going on. I didn't even have to ask. I just gave him a questioning expression.

"Gina called," he explained. Gina was my publicist, so my brows furrowed the instant I heard her name. He paused, and his expression changed as he tilted his head at me. "Were you crying?"

"Yeah but it was a good cry, what's going on? What did Gina say?"

He shook his head. "It's not that big of a deal. You and I just got photographed at the airport and Gina caught wind of it and called to make sure we knew."

"Already?" I asked. "That was just like three hours ago. How'd Gina know about it?"

"It's nothing big. Somebody took a few pictures of us at the airport and tagged you on their social media. Obviously, you had on your hat and everything, but Gina said it was a pretty clear picture of your face and that it had had some shares and stuff. She said she saw to it that you weren't tagged anymore, whatever that means, but she just wanted to make sure we knew what was going on."

Daniel paused and glanced outside through the window. "I really don't think anyone is going to bother you out here. I just figured I'd have you go ahead and come inside."

I leaned forward, collapsing onto his chest, and he held me and rubbed my back lovingly. "Was everything okay out there?" he asked, referring again to my tears.

"Yeah," I whispered. "Your mom was just being really sweet and telling me how much she loved you."

"She does love me," Daniel said. "But I didn't expect her to take you out here and start gushing about it."

"She wasn't gushing," I said. "And even if she was, I'm glad about it. It was sweet. I really love your mom—your whole family. Is it okay for me to say that?"

"Yes. They love you too," he said. "And I think Ivy was slightly excited to see you."

I laughed. "She was so cute when I told her I was going to her graduation."

"What'd she say?"

"It's not what she said. It's just that she started paddling her feet like she was swimming in a pool."

"What?" Daniel asked in a confused tone like he obviously couldn't picture it.

"Nothing," I said. "She was just really cute and sweet. And she invited us to a graduation party she's having at your cousin's house."

"Oh Lord, I'm sure she did," Daniel said.

"Even if we don't end up going to that, I'm really looking forward to seeing Shelby again and meeting the rest of your family." I pulled back to stare at him, and he glanced down at me, wearing that gorgeous smile.

"I'm glad," he said. "They want to meet you, too."

"What about Owen?" I whispered.

"What about him?"

"What'd he say about me being here? Does he know I'm your girlfriend?"

Daniel's grin broadened at my question. "Owen's really happy you're here," he said.

I couldn't quit staring at his teeth. His smile was so irresistible that I wanted to kiss him constantly. I stretched upward and snagged a quick kiss, regretting that I couldn't stand there and repeat the process about fifty more times. He kissed me back before squeezing my hand to let me know we should head into the house before we got carried away.

We joined the rest of his family in the living room and spent the next hour or so talking to them. They had all pitched in with helping Shelby fix up her new house. The whole family donated their time and some of their extra furnishings to the project, and Ivy filled them all in on what Shelby was putting where.

It was just a normal evening for the Bishops— one where they sat around and caught each other up on what had been going on in their lives during the past few days. I was overjoyed that they welcomed me into their family conversation without feeling the need to filter what they said or even try to impress me.

I loved them all, but there was already a special place in my heart for Owen. It wasn't out of pity, either, because honestly, I couldn't see where he was at any detriment in life because of the injuries he got in the accident. His scar was actually becoming on him, and the fact that he was wearing jeans made it impossible to tell that there was anything different about his leg.

My warm feelings toward Owen weren't a result of me feeling bad for him—it wasn't that at all. If anything, it was out of gratefulness. I knew Daniel had been deeply concerned about Owen's feelings all these years, which was why he didn't date. They had both experienced pain and heartache as a result of the accident, and I was truly sorry for that, but the end result was that Daniel remained single long enough for me to find him. He unintentionally saved himself for me, and for that, I was eternally grateful.

Daniel was a diamond in the rough—a true, pure soul with a heart of gold—and I knew deep in my heart how fortunate I was to call him mine. Granted, it wasn't all about me. God, no doubt, used the accident to affect the lives of the boys and everyone around them, but I still somehow felt that Owen's sacrifice translated into my gain, and I had a special fondness for him because of that.

It was almost 9pm when Daniel told his parents he and I should be getting home. We thanked them for the meal and made plans to go by Bishop Motorcycles within the next couple of days so that I could take a tour.

Owen was ready to leave as well, so he walked outside with us. The two of them talked about one of their family friends who had a swimming hole on their property and the fact that Daniel should take me out there. I had never gone swimming in a "hole" before, but I figured it might be fun, so I just smiled and went along with it.

Daniel and I stood next to his motorcycle, and Owen walked toward his truck, but turned and leaned against it instead of getting inside. He smiled at us. Daniel came to stand behind me, wrapping his arms protectively around my shoulders. This made Owen's smile widen as he shook his head.

"I can't believe my eyes," Owen said, pretending to rub his eyes with his fists as if he was seeing things. "I thought Daniel would never find a woman who suited him."

"I had to trick him into liking me," I said, turning in Daniel's arms so that I could stare at him from over my shoulder. "I had to fake sick so that he'd come take care of me." We both knew that I had not been faking it, but that's just what came out.

Daniel smiled at me before looking at Owen. "Plus, she showed off," Daniel said. "She danced and sang these songs into a microphone and had a bunch of people cheer for her and stuff."

I rolled my eyes at him and we all laughed.

"Seriously, though," Owen said. "I'm not sure any less of a woman could have managed to get his attention, so I'm glad it worked out."

He was being sincere, and I smiled, feeling a bit shy and speechless.

"I probably don't deserve such a compliment, but thank you," I said. "I definitely feel like I'm the one who scored in this situation."

"You really did," Owen said. "I know he's my brother and everything, but I'm not just being biased... he's a good man."

"He likes you a little bit, too," I said.

Owen gave me a confident smile and shrug as he turned to open the door of his truck. "It runs in the family, I guess. We like each other." He climbed into his truck, and I ran over so that I could catch him and give him a hug before he closed the door.

He seemed surprised but thankful that I would do such a thing and he leaned over to hug me from the driver's seat. "I'm glad you came to Memphis," he said.

"Me too," I said. "I'm so happy to meet you guys."

We stared at each other with sincere smiles before he closed the door. I stepped back as he started the truck, rolling his window down in the process.

"I'll see you soon," he said. He gave us a two-fingered salute as he backed up and headed out of the driveway.

I turned and stared at Daniel once we were alone.

He laughed at my wide-eyed expression.

I was on the very verge of mentioning how amazing it was that I could not tell Owen wore a prosthetic leg even though I knew it was there and had been looking for it, but I reconsidered saying that.

"What?" he asked, chuckling at my expression.

"I love him," I said instead, which was still the truth. "I love all of them—your whole family, but Owen... I don't know. I just like him so much."

"Me too," Daniel said. "He's good to me. He's never once made me feel..." Daniel hesitated, handing me my helmet. "He's just a really good person."

I smiled as I put on my helmet. Part of me wanted to say more, but I stayed quiet while I searched for the right words.

"While you and Mom were on the porch, he told Dad and me that he was talking to someone."

"Who, Owen?"

Daniel nodded.

"*Talking*, talking?" I asked, tilting my head at him as I fastened my helmet strap. "Like a girlfriend?"

Daniel nodded again. "He definitely didn't say the word girlfriend. He said he'd been talking to someone, but then he got quiet and seemed really secretive about it."

"Did he say who she was?"

Daniel shook his head. "Dad and I both tried to ask him questions, but he wouldn't say any more. It seemed like he almost regretted mentioning it."

"Oh, now I'm curious," I said.

Daniel smiled at me. He grabbed the handlebars in such a way that I knew he was about to start the motorcycle. I stood back while he started the engine and then gestured for me to get on. He glanced over his shoulder, waiting for me to get situated. I stretched upward, placing a kiss on his cheek.

"You ready?" he asked.

I gave him a nod, and off we went.

Chapter 19

Ivy's graduation snuck up on us.

The old saying about time flying when you're having fun must be true because the first week I spent in Memphis seemed more like two days. I had some friends in Nashville, and Daniel and I spent one night there so that I could connect with a couple of them.

We also swam in the swimming hole, which wasn't nearly as intimidating as I imagined. It was basically a big pond in the woods with trails, docks, diving boards, and rope swings. It was on a nice piece of private property owned by friends of Daniel's family, and they let us have a big family party out there. Ivy was graduating high school, and a few family members had birthdays in May (along with Mother's Day, obviously), so Rose and Jesse invited the extended family and made it a big, impromptu Bishop get together with barbeque sandwiches and cake and ice cream.

Daniel had a lot of family in Memphis—more than I even knew about. His mom had brothers who had kids, and they all came out along with Daniel's Uncle Gray and Aunt Jane. I got to meet Daniel's great-grandparents who they called Pa and Nana and both sets of his grandparents, (Ivy and Michael) and (Jacob and Alice). I didn't count, but there were what must have been thirty or forty people out there, and they were all wonderful.

Of course, I got to catch up with Shelby, which was nice. She had gone to hair school and had a passion for doing hair and makeup. She was currently working as a stylist for a local news station and had aspirations to get into more elaborate makeup design for movies and television. She had done a few things locally and had plans to work on a couple of music videos in Nashville soon.

She had a real love for it, and thought of it as an art form. Several times during our conversation, she reached out and touched the side of my hair, pulling it up as if imagining it being styled this way or that. I loved that she felt comfortable and familiar enough with me to do that. She and I were friends instantly.

It was during our afternoon at the family barbecue when Shelby and I made plans for Ivy's graduation. We brought up the fact that I would like to go to Ivy's graduation party but didn't really want to be hassled. Word had gotten out that I was in Memphis, and I had been photographed by the paparazzi a few times when we were out and about.

By the end of our conversation, Shelby hatched an idea that would solve everything and let me enjoy Ivy's big night in secret. She said she could give me such a convincing disguise that I would be able to go to Ivy's graduation and the after party without anyone even knowing it was me.

The graduation ceremony started at 6pm, and we had plans to eat dinner with the family afterward. Ivy said she told her friends from school that the party at Shelby's would get started at 9, and if all went well, I would be able to go to all three activities without being noticed or bothered. It was a tall order, but Shelby seemed convinced that she could pull it off.

Shelby came to Daniel's house that afternoon at 3pm to help me get dressed. She didn't tell me what she was doing, but when I saw the polyester clothing, gray wig, and the walking cane, I put two and two together.

I honestly couldn't believe the results. I had never been dressed up to look like an old lady before. I had put on my share of costumes over the years, I had never once been made to look like a much older version of myself.

I stared at my reflection in the mirror, thinking Shelby was an absolute genius and there was no way anyone would know it was me. I barely knew it was me. I wasn't wearing a mask, but I might as well have been with how different I looked.

I touched my own face, wondering how the world she made my skin look I like it had aged fifty years. The salt and pepper wig put it over the top. It all looked natural and understated. I knew no one would recognize me.

"Do you like it?" she asked, standing behind me as I checked out my reflection.

"How'd you do this?" I asked in awe.

"They're just little silicone pads that I glued on strategically. Are they comfortable? Do you feel like you can smile and talk like normal? It's the first time I've used those things, but I've watched a lot of tutorials and I've really been wanting to try them."

I stretched my face, being careful not to make any extreme movements. I tried a smile, and had to laugh at myself.

"I think it's perfect," I said in my best imitation of an old lady.

This made Shelby crack up laughing. "Don't forget to move a little slower than usual," Shelby said. "You don't have to limp or anything, but just don't walk around doing cartwheels."

She patted me on the butt, which was padded so much that I barely felt her. She and I had been in Daniel's bedroom getting ready. I was staying in a different bedroom, but his master had an attached bathroom, so we had set up shop in there. She went to the door and opened it.

"Daniel!" she called. "Can you please look after Aunt Edna tonight?"

I tried not to laugh as I braced myself for Daniel to come around the corner. I was so nervous to see his reaction that I could hardly stand it.

"I'm going to go get myself dressed," Shelby said before Daniel even came around the corner.

She grinned at me and took off for the other room. "Aunt Edna's waiting for you," I heard her say when she reached the hall.

My heart was beating a million miles an hour when Daniel came to stand in the doorway. It had only been a couple of hours since I had seen him, but I was all amped up with nervous anticipation.

He was the most handsome thing I had ever seen. He had on dark slacks with a coordinating shirt that was tucked in with a matching belt and shoes. Everything was freshly ironed and super-sharp. He had shaved his face for the occasion, and he was utterly dashing.

I was so busy noticing how gorgeous he was that it took me a second to realize that he was wearing a serious, almost intense expression as he stared at me.

"Are you kidding me right now?" was the first thing he said. "Are you seriously my Courtney?"

I smiled and performed a slight bow.

"Where did you get that stuff?" he asked.

"Shelby brought it over," I said. "I think she said the outfit belonged to Nana's mom. The wig and makeup were Shelby's. I think she might have bought them just for this. I'm glad you reminded me. I need to settle up with her for everything."

Daniel stepped closer to me as I was talking. He stared at me with a concerned expression as if trying to figure something out. "You *sound* like Courtney," he said, standing right in front of me and looking directly into my eyes.

"That's because I am Courtney," I said with a little smile.

Daniel could hardly recognize me even when he got right up next to me and stared into my eyes. I knew if he had so much trouble no one else would be able to recognize me either.

I went by "Aunt Edna" all evening, sitting next to Daniel like he was my caretaker. We held hands during moments when it could go unnoticed, but otherwise we behaved as if I was his great-aunt. The Bishops were all great actors and went along with it without skipping a beat. They seemed so convinced that I was Aunt Edna that I thought a few of them might actually believe I was a distant relative they had forgotten about.

We went to the graduation ceremony and then out to eat with about twenty family members before going back to Daniel's parents' house. Daniel gave me countless opportunities to wrap up the evening so that I could get out of my disguise, but I quite enjoyed flying under the radar as Aunt Edna and was excited about going to the party.

He and I got to Shelby's house at 9pm, and we were blown away by the number of people who were already there. Shelby lived in a residential neighborhood, and there were so many cars that we had to park a block away. On the way to her house Daniel and I talked about the number of people who were there. Both of us were protective of Shelby and were instantly a bit on edge about the turnout.

Shelby was by no means providing alcohol for the partygoers, but it was obvious to us as soon as we walked in the door that most of them were drinking. They weren't doing it openly, but they were loud and raucous. The place was completely packed with graduating seniors and their friends.

We found Shelby and Ivy in the kitchen. Daniel had about all he could handle of the rowdy boys who were present in the group, and he was ready to start kicking people out as soon as we got there. Shelby insisted that she was fine with it, though, and said she would rather Ivy have a party at her house than go to one at some other, unsafe location.

Daniel and I wound up staying for a couple of hours. There was one guy who was especially unruly, and Daniel wasn't comfortable leaving while he was still there. He had gotten worse and worse throughout the night, and I could see Daniel's wheels turning.

At one point, he even asked Ivy how exactly she knew him. She told him that he was a football player named Blake who had graduated a couple of years before but was still friends with Ivy's friends.

Several times, throughout the night, the guy had offended someone in earshot of Daniel, and finally, it was too much.

He was standing with a group of boys, all laughing and joking around. Daniel and I had caught sight of Ivy and were watching as she walked toward us. Blake reached out and goosed Ivy on her rear end as she passed him. She shot him a look of disapproval, but he just gave her an innocent stare and pointed at the guy who was standing next to him.

That was all Daniel could take. I knew the guy was about to regret what he had just done.

"I'll be right back," Daniel said.

He left my side to head in their direction, and I watched closely, secretly hoping that he would walk over there and punch that guy square in the jaw. There were so many people present at the party that I couldn't hear what they were saying. Daniel confronted Blake who, in turn, bowed up to him getting in his face like he could actually do something in spite of the fact that Daniel was much taller, broader, and tougher looking.

Blake patted his own chest and flinched like he was about to hit Daniel, and then next thing I knew, Daniel turned as he performed a smooth, sweeping move that easily flipped the guy into the air, landing him flat on his back.

Everyone standing around stepped back and started pointing at them. I smiled at the way Daniel calmly yet forcefully handled the situation. He stooped to say something to the guy who was wincing in pain from the fall.

I had seen Trevor take similar action a couple of times, but not like Daniel. He was so calm and in control yet tough and impassive that I felt a wave of desire for him.

I was happy that he was the type of guy who took up for his sister and wouldn't be disrespected by young men who were being out of line. Daniel talked with his sister for a minute after the whole thing went down, and then he made his way over to me.

"Are you about ready?" he asked as he approached.

I nodded.

He turned to Shelby. "We're gonna walk Blake and his ride out to their truck, so they won't be bothering you anymore. Ivy said everyone else knows to be out of here by midnight. I'm a phone call away and so is your dad if you have any trouble getting them to leave."

"I won't," Shelby said. "Dad's already text me ten times. He said he's coming by at midnight to make sure everyone's headed home. They're all being cool except for that guy, anyway."

"Well, he's leaving," Daniel said. "So you won't have to worry about him."

I hugged Shelby and thanked her for making it possible for me to enjoy the evening with no one knowing who I was. Daniel smiled at us before taking the keys out of his pocket and offering me his arm.

"It's way past your bedtime, Aunt Edna," he said.

"I don't know how you managed to put that dad-blasted hooligan on his back like that," I said in my best old lady voice, causing him to smile. I pinched his cheek. "You sure are an athletic young man, Daniel. I'm so proud of you."

Chapter 20

My love for Daniel was like an avalanche.

I met him, and one little piece of my resolve broke away. Then he came to Dallas, and then to California, and again, little pieces of my resolve began to crumble and fall away. Then I spent time getting to know him from across the miles, and more and more tiny pieces started falling away.

And then there was Memphis.

My time in Memphis shattered me into smithereens and sent me freefalling into the gorgeous abyss called love.

I loved Daniel before I ever went to Tennessee, but something about meeting his family and getting to know his roots sealed the deal in such a way that I just couldn't leave there and go back to my life in California.

Yet, there I was at the end of my two-week trip.

I would fly back to L.A. the following day.

But I knew in my heart that it wasn't an option.

I had no plan other than not sticking to the current plan.

Daniel and I had just finished eating dinner at his parents'. They all knew that I was flying home the following day, so it was a sort of 'farewell to Courtney' gathering with some of the extended family.

It was a beautiful afternoon, and a group of us went for a ride before going to his parents' house for dinner. There were seven motorcycles in all. Some were carrying passengers and others weren't, so I think there were a total of ten or twelve people who went on the excursion. I had done some cool things in my life, but traveling in a big group with the very family who made the beautiful machines we were riding was perhaps the coolest.

I felt like I was a part of the most awesome motorcycle gang that had ever walked the face of the earth—and we didn't even have matching jackets.

I smiled at the thought of it.

"What are you smiling at?" Daniel asked as we walked into his house at the end of the evening. We had just gotten back from dinner, and I couldn't stop thinking about everything we had just done and wishing I could reenact it every night for the rest of my life.

I reached out for Daniel and we wrapped our arms around each other as we walked.

"I was thinking about getting matching jackets," I said. "That was so fun riding in a big group like that. I wish we all had jackets like the T-Birds and Pink Ladies."

"You can be my Pink Lady any day," Daniel said, unlocking his door. He held it open for me and we walked inside.

"How about today?" I asked.

He tossed his keys onto the counter and I swung myself into his arms, forcing him to catch me.

"How about every day?" he asked, smiling at me when I landed in his arms.

"I thought you'd never ask," I said.

We stared at each other with completely serious expressions for several long seconds.

"Never ask what?" he asked, finally.

"Ask me to be your Pink Lady everyday."

"You already know I want that," he said. "Or did you just need me to call you a Pink Lady?"

I shook my head. "It has nothing to do with the Pink Ladies and T-Birds," I said. "It's the *every day* part I'm talking about."

Daniel wrapped his hands around my waist pulling me close to him. "Courtney, baby, you must know by now that I want you to be mine every day. I would feel terrible if I hadn't done enough to assure you of that."

"What about tomorrow?" I asked.

"You'll be mine tomorrow just the same as you were mine today and yesterday."

I loved it when he called me 'his'. It wasn't the first time he had done it, and each time the word sent a rush of anticipation through me.

"I know, but I won't be here tomorrow," I said. I furrowed my eyebrows and gave him a disgruntled expression that made him smile.

"Yeah, but that doesn't mean you won't be mine," he said.

I wrapped my arms around his midsection, hugging him tightly. I loved the way his body felt— the way muscles lined his back and sides. I wanted to feel him pressed up against me like this for the rest of my life. I never wanted to let him go.

"Can't you see that I'm trying to get you to beg me to stay?" I asked.

His smile faded and he regarded me seriously. "Courtney, if I thought for *one second* that begging you to stay would make you do it, then I would beg. I would have no shame. I would fall to my knees and beg, right here right now."

My heart began racing because I could see that he was serious. He honestly thought that I had to go back to California—or that I wanted to.

I lifted my hand and touched his face. His dark eyes were so endless and mysterious that I felt like there were elements of him I might never know.

"Ask me to stay with you, and I will, Daniel," I whispered, still touching his face.

"Stay, Courtney," he said without hesitation.

He said it so earnestly that I had no other choice but to smile. "Do you mean it?" I asked.

His expression shifted to one of slight confusion like he couldn't believe I would even ask such a thing. "Of course I mean it," he said incredulously. "I am so sorry you even feel the need to ask that," he added sweetly. "I want you to stay with me. I want you to stay tomorrow, and the next day, and the one after that. Stay by my side and never leave me,

Courtney. Just go ahead and marry me and wake up next to me every single morning. If I had things my way, that's what would happen."

"Then, let's do it your way," I said.

My heart was about to beat out of my chest because I meant every word I was saying, and I knew Daniel did also. We were on the verge of making a real true commitment to each other, and we both knew it.

"I love you," I said. "I don't want to be apart. I don't want to leave tomorrow. I don't want to leave ever. I mean, I want to take trips and do stuff, but I want you with me."

"Do you understand what you're saying?" he asked.

I nodded. "Perfectly."

"What?" he asked.

"I hope we're saying I'll cancel my flight tomorrow and just go ahead and rearrange plans for the rest of my life—that I'll just go ahead and marry you and be your lady for good."

"Can you really do that?" Daniel asked.

"Can *you*?"

"Yeah, but you have a whole life and persona and everything over in California."

I was still barely touching his cheek with my fingertips. "Do I? Do I really? As it stands, the idea of leaving Memphis seems more dreadful than the idea of not returning to L.A. I know I have a life over there, but I'd rather not go back to it if it means leaving you, Daniel."

Daniel put his fingers to his ear and made a somewhat confused expression like he was trying to discern what he was hearing. "The words you're saying right now are the most precious, unreal words I've ever heard in my life. They are entering my ears and then somehow miraculously causing things to happen inside of me. It's amazing to me that words formed with your mouth and spoken into the air can cause a physical shift in my body like this. Please say I'm hearing you correctly when you say you're not getting on a plane tomorrow. Please say you're staying with me."

"I am," I said, smiling.

"Seriously?" he asked.

I nodded. "I don't want to leave you," I whispered.

"I don't want you to leave, either," he said.

"Let's not do it, then."

"Great. Stay," he said.

"Fine. I will."

The hint of a grin touched the corners of his mouth, but otherwise we just stood there and stared at each other.

"Marry me," he said.

"Okay."

"Okay?" he asked.

I nodded. "Yes."

He scanned my face as if searching my expression to make sure I was serious.

"When?" I asked.

"Yesterday," he said.

"Yesterday's gone," I said. "How about tomorrow?"

He smiled. "Don't tempt me," he said. "My granddad's a pastor. I could seriously make that happen. (a pause) Courtney."

"What?"

"I am a hundred percent serious right now."

"So am I, Daniel. So am I. My heart is about to beat out of my chest right now. I'm super serious. I want to be with you every day for forever."

"Let's do it, then," he whispered. "We don't really have to get married tomorrow, but let's do it. Let's do it soon."

I nodded. "Okay."

"Really?" he asked.

"Really," I said.

"So, you're not flying home tomorrow?" he asked, clarifying.

"I'm already home," I said.

Daniel's expression changed when I said that. It was subtle, but there was a change, and it caused warmth to spread through my body. He realized how serious I was. He realized I was giving him ownership of my heart, and he smiled at me like he was up for the challenge. He scanned my face with his gorgeous dark eyes, taking in every inch as if memorizing it.

I knew he was going to kiss me, and I got a tingling sensation in my lower abdomen as I waited for him to do it. I stared at his mouth waiting desperately for him to come closer—for him to close the remaining few inches that separated us.

"I'm yours, Daniel." I whispered the words, hoping that would send him over the edge, and it worked.

Daniel kissed me. He started with a couple of gentle, tender kisses, and then he opened his mouth to me, kissing me more deeply than he ever had before. He kissed me so fully and deeply that the action of it conveyed a promise of things to come.

I told Daniel Bishop that he owned my heart, and he kissed me as if he fully understood what that ownership meant. There was such urgency and passion in his kiss that it felt as though we were sharing something different than we ever had before.

I wrapped my hand around the back of his head, holding him closely and letting him know this was exactly what I wanted. He somehow poured love, tenderness, and possessive protectiveness into me during that kiss and I received it gratefully, letting him know with muted whimpers and clinched fists that I was his just like he was mine.

It hit me during that kiss that I was the only woman to ever receive that type of affection from Daniel, and the thought of it made a swelling sensation happen inside me. I held him tightly, conveying the fact that I ached desperately for more of him, and he kissed me deeply for a few more charged moments before breaking the kiss and pulling back.

I let out a moan of disappointment as he broke contact, and he smiled before letting his lips touch mine again like he just couldn't resist. He kissed me three or four more times, all with great gentleness, before finally pulling back. I held onto his shirt with tightly clinched fists because I couldn't bear to let him go.

"We better get married," I said breathlessly.

Epilogue

Daniel and I took a few months to plan for the wedding. I didn't want anything too elaborate, but we talked about it and decided to take our time with the arrangements. The media would have had a field day with a spur of the moment wedding. It wasn't that I cared what other people thought necessarily, but I loved Daniel so much that I wanted to be taken seriously about it. I went back and forth on that quite a bit, but I ultimately chose to be a little patient.

We decided to have the ceremony in California. The weather was predictably good, and we both liked the idea doing it outside on the beach. I had several picturesque places in mind, and Daniel easily agreed since he knew his family would fly out to join us for the occasion.

I wasn't sad about moving away from Los Angeles, but I did have a lot of friends there and was happy about them being able to come to the wedding since it would sort of double as my going away party. I hadn't officially made a statement about my career, but those closest to me knew that I would, at least, be taking a long hiatus from touring. I had been at it for so long that I was more than ready for the change and thankful to Daniel for being there at just the right moment to make the adjustment seem natural.

In the weeks following my trip to Memphis, Daniel and I did some traveling. Everything we did was impromptu. I would say something like, *"I've always wanted to see Stonehenge."* And he would reply with, *"Let's go."*

We went to England, Brazil, and Alaska, and all three of the trips were completely unplanned. I got to meet his brother, Wes, when we went to England. I had seen him before using Skype, but he was the only Bishop that I hadn't had the chance to meet in person, so that made our trip to England especially nice.

Daniel and I loved each other and it showed. He could often be seen with his arm around my shoulders while I snuggled into his protective embrace. We had been photographed quite a bit in positions like that during our travels. A few publications ran articles on how I fell in love with my bodyguard and a couple of others found out who Daniel was and speculated that I was dating motorcycle royalty.

It was for this reason that my publicist recommended that I give the tell-all story to one publication so that we could avoid any more rumors or confusion.

People Magazine did a story on us, taking photos of Daniel training martial arts at work and some with his family at Bishop Motorcycles. Elvis the bird even got his picture taken for the spread.

I bought a house with a bunch of property on the outskirts of Memphis, and they took pictures of Daniel and me out there. It was a really good, honest article that included some of the details about how we met and the fact that we had plans to get married in the near future.

I went to California two weeks before Daniel, so I got to see the article before he did. I texted him pictures of it with a note that said, "This only makes me miss you more," which was the absolute truth.

I didn't love being away from him, but the old adage about absence making the heart grow fonder seemed to be true, and it felt like I loved him now more than ever.

Daniel thought about coming with me, but he had already taken off a lot of work so that we could travel and he knew we had another trip coming up with the honeymoon. I had been busy in California, anyway. I had a lot of things to get in order for the wedding and my move, and the days passed quickly.

Trevor had taken a position with a country star named Brie Ellerbe, so Daniel paired me up with another guy named Sam for the two weeks that I would be alone in L.A. All the guys at Alpha were dependably professional, so it was no surprise that Sam did a great job.

Great job or not, he wasn't Daniel.

I absolutely could not wait to see my man and counted the minutes until it happened.

Daniel, along with roughly twenty members of his family and a couple of his friends, flew to California for the big event. My mom and step-dad would be there along with about fifty of my friends. I initially wanted it to be even more intimate than that, but with all the industry connections I had made over the years, I already felt like I was leaving a lot of people out.

Daniel and the crew from Memphis flew in the day before the wedding. We saw each other, but we intentionally made it brief. Daniel and his immediate family were staying in my friend's beautiful beachfront home in Malibu, which was also the location of the wedding. His back yard was the ocean, and he had access to a small, private lagoon that looked like something out of a movie. It actually had been used in movies.

Anyway, William was nice enough to host our wedding, and he even offered a few of his bedrooms to the groom and his family the night before. A few stayed at my house, but everyone else stayed in a nearby hotel.

I hired Nina and Jake to do my styling for the event. Shelby had stayed at my house, so she was there while I was getting dressed, and they all had a great time talking shop and scheming about how to make me look my best.

I showed Jake and Nina photos from the time Shelby made me look like Aunt Edna, and they both got the biggest kick out of that. They promised to introduce Shelby to some of their industry contacts at the wedding, and I was pleased that they liked each other and got along so well.

I was so nervous that the hours leading up to the wedding felt like one big dream. The ceremony itself felt like a dream as well.

There were roughly seventy people in attendance, but there may as well have been none because I only had eyes for Daniel. I don't even remember walking toward him on the beach. I knew I had crossed space to get to him, but I honestly don't remember doing it. One second, I was hidden away with Denise while she whispered affirmations in my ear, and the next, I was standing right next to Daniel, holding his hands and staring into his endless eyes.

He smiled warmly at me. "You're so beautiful," he said.

"How did I get here?" I whispered.

"Same way I did, I guess."

His granddad was officiating the ceremony, and he just stood there watching us look at each other. So did everyone else, I assumed. I really didn't notice what anyone else was doing—I only noticed Daniel. He was dressed nicely in navy slacks with a matching vest and a bowtie. It was just formal enough for a beach wedding, and I stared at him, thinking he was the most striking man I had ever seen.

"I'm marrying you," I whispered, still gripping his hands.

His grin widened. "It's a good thing," he said. "Because that's what all these people are expecting you to do."

"I'm glad we're doing this," I said.

"Me too."

"I love you," I said.

"I love you too."

The wind was blowing, and Daniel let go of my hand just long enough to reach up and tuck a piece of hair behind my ear.

"Thank you," I said.

"You're the most beautiful thing ever."

I smiled shyly at him and bit my lip. "You are too," I said. "Handsome, I mean. I missed you so much."

"I had plans to start talking right when she walked up here," Jacob said, speaking loudly so that the whole group could hear him over the sounds of the wind and crashing waves. "But they're just so sweet that I had to stand here and listen to them talk to each other. I feel like they're already saying their vows."

We turned to Jacob and he smiled genuinely at us before making eye contact with the rest of the group. He took a second to gather his thoughts.

"I've watched my grandson go through a lot in his young life," he said.

He spoke slowly and proudly, like he was saying the words as they came to his mind and he was choosing them carefully.

"There's a verse in the Bible that says suffering produces endurance, endurance produces character, and character produces hope."

He paused and glanced at Daniel sweetly.

"Over the years, I've watched that promise come to life in my grandson. I watched him grow, change, and develop character—unshakable character. Now, as I stand here and look at these two, I see hope. I see a future. I see true and determined love, and I couldn't be prouder of them or the decision they've made to become one today. It's a great honor to see God's promise revealed so clearly in the life of my grandson and to get to be a part of this beautiful and significant step in his life."

Daniel and I both had our backs to the crowd, and I was glad for that, because my eyes were filled with tears. Jacob stopped talking and smiled at me with tears in his own eyes. And then, in a very unorthodox move, he reached forward and wrapped his arms around me.

"We love you, Courtney," he said into my ear. "We're so thankful God brought you into Daniel's life."

"Uh-huh," I whimpered, nodding as I hugged him back. "Me too."

He let go of me and spoke for another five minutes about love, commitment, family, and gratefulness.

Daniel kept his arm around me the whole time and I rested my face on his chest since we were so very comfortable that way.

Before I knew it, he was given permission to kiss me, and I turned and looked at him. He gave me a mischievous grin, which implied that this kiss was only the beginning. This caused a whole flood of emotions and anticipation to rise inside of me. He put his lips right next to mine but didn't let them touch. I held him by the arms, squeezing him.

"This is it," I whispered.

"Yep."

"I love yo—"

I started to say the phrase, but Daniel let his lips touch mine before I could get it out. I took a shaky breath as we kissed, realizing once again how very much I loved the soft feel of his perfect lips. He let them linger on mine for a few brief seconds before he pulled back and gave me an easy smile.

"I love you too," he said.

The End
(Till book 5)

Not only that, but we rejoice in our sufferings, knowing that suffering produces endurance, and endurance produces character, and character produces hope, and hope does not put us to shame, because God's love has been poured into our hearts through the Holy Spirit who has been given to us.

Romans 5:3-5

Thanks to my team – Chris, Coda, Jan, and Glenda

Made in the USA
Middletown, DE
06 July 2021

43648132R00130